A Wreath Of Indian Stories

By

A. L. O. E.

A Wreath Of Indian Stories
by A. L. O. E.

ISBN: 978-93-59956-79-4
Published by

DOUBLE 9 BOOKS
2/13-B, Ansari Road
Daryaganj, New Delhi – 110002
info@double9books.com
www.double9books.com
Tel. 011-40042856

ABOUT THE AUTHOR

A. L. O. E, which stands for "A Lady of England," turned into the pseudonym of the prolific nineteenth-century English writer Charlotte Maria Tucker. A devout Christian and philanthropist, Tucker's writings broadly speaking focused young readers, and he or she received reputation for her ethical and academic literature. One of her remarkable works is "A Wreath of Indian Stories." This collection of stories is a satisfying combination of adventure, moral classes, and an exploration of Indian tradition. A. L. O. E's writing fashion is characterised by way of its readability and an inherent choice to instill values and virtues in her readers. "A Wreath of Indian Stories" is not any exception, as it weaves collectively testimonies set in India, introducing readers to the vibrant and various tapestry of the Indian subcontinent. Through her tales, A. L. O. E aimed to teach young readers about the world past their instantaneous surroundings and sell a sense of empathy and understanding for specific cultures. Her testimonies regularly featured sturdy ethical messages, encouraging kindness, compassion, and a feel of responsibility toward others. In "A Wreath of Indian Stories," A. L. O. E's skillful storytelling transports readers to the fascinating international of India even as presenting precious lifestyles instructions, making her works both enjoyable and instructive for young audiences. A. L. O. E's literary legacy is still liked for its contribution to children's literature and its commitment to nurturing young minds with stories of journey and virtue.

CONTENTS

Preface

The following stories have been written by A. L. O. E. since her arrival in India, for the use of native readers. It is deemed most desirable by those who thoroughly know the people, that their minds should be trained in the first principles of morality, as well as of religion, by means of amusing fictions, as they are particularly fond of stories. A. L. O. E. desires, therefore, to devote her pen to the service of the land of her adoption, as there are, comparatively speaking, hardly any writers who enjoy the advantage of having the peculiar habits and failings of Hindus, Mohammedans, Sikhs, and native converts, perpetually brought before their notice, as is, or should be, the case with a member of a missionary band.

If her little "Indian Stories" be acceptable in her dear native land, she will be thankful; but the object which she chiefly aims at is to write in a way to amuse, and through amusement to instruct, the people of the country of her adoption.

As stories placed in the hands of Oriental readers would be comparatively useless unless written in an Oriental style, and describing scenes and customs familiar to natives, A. L. O. E. has tried to adopt such a style, and depict such scenes. When she reviewed her work, with the mental question, "What would be thought of this in England?" she felt how fanciful and affected her writings might appear to European readers, and almost gave up all idea of sending them home. And yet, as quaint and often grotesque ornaments brought from the East are not despised in Britain because they are unlike our own manufactures, but are sometimes even prized for their very quaintness, it is possible that a few of A. L. O. E.'s Oriental stories may not be unacceptable in her native land. They may even serve to awaken a little interest in a vast country like India, where a Native Church is struggling against surrounding evil influences, — a Church as yet small compared with the myriads of its opponents, yet gaining strength year by year. That infant Church needs tender care and indulgence from those who have been brought up in a land bathed in the light of Christianity, — a land where children are taught almost from the cradle the value of honesty and truth, and where little is known of the fearful difficulties and trials which beset converts to the pure faith of the gospel.

I
The Radiant Robe

Fagir, the government clerk, sat in his house, when the work of the day was over. He had partaken of his evening meal; he had smoked his hookah;[1] his bodily frame was at ease, but his mind was working with many thoughts. His wife was beside him—Kasiti, the gentle and obedient. Kasiti had long ago embraced the gospel and become a Christian in heart, but many months had passed before her husband had suffered her to be baptized. He had chidden her, and she had not answered again; he had been harsh, and she had been loving. Kasiti[2] had made her faith appear beautiful by her life, and her patience had at length won the victory. Fagir had not only consented to his wife's baptism, but he had read her Bible; he had searched its pages diligently, comparing the Old Testament with the New. And now Fagir's intellect was convinced of the truth of Christianity; light dawned upon his soul, but it was as light without warmth. Fagir believed in Christ as the Messiah, but refused still to receive Him as a Sacrifice for sin.

"Such a sacrifice is not needed; at least, for those who walk uprightly and in the fear of God," said Fagir to Kasiti, who was seated at his feet, with a Bible on her knees. "It would be mockery for such as I am to repeat what the Christians are taught to say—'God be merciful to me, a sinner.' I, at least, am no sinner, but a just and upright man, even judged by the laws contained in that Bible. I can hold my head erect before God and man; for I serve God with fasting and prayer, and man have I never wronged, but have bestowed large alms on the poor."

It was not for Kasiti to reply; she read to herself in silence; but the thought of her heart was, "Had not Christ died for sinners, there would have been no heaven for me."

The evening was hot; the motion of the gently-moving punkah[3] disposed Fagir to sleep. His eyes gradually closed, and slumber stole over him where he sat, reclining on soft cushions. And as the weary man slept he dreamed, and his dream was as vivid as the realities of daily life could be.

Behold in his dream a beautiful angel appeared unto Fagir. A crown of light was on the head of the messenger of Heaven; glory was as a mantle around him, and when he shook his silvery wings a shower of stars seemed to fall upon earth. Fagir trembled at the sight of the pure and holy being who floated in the air before him without touching the ground with his shining feet.

"O Fagir, thou art bidden to the banquet of Paradise!" said the angel; and his voice was as music at night. "Receive this white robe, in which, if it retain its whiteness, thou mayst be meet to appear in the presence of the great King. But beware of sin; for every sin shall be as a stain on thy robe. Keep it white for but *one day*, and all the joys of Paradise shall be thine eternal reward."

As the angel spake, he cast round the form of Fagir a radiant robe, white as the snow on the mountains. Then the angel touched the broad border of the robe, and on the border appeared in letters of gold, *Fear God, and keep his commandments* (Eccles. xii. 13). Fagir gazed in wonder on the inscription; but even as he gazed it faded away. He turned to look on the angel, but behold! the bright messenger had vanished. Nothing remained but the pure white robe, which Fagir still wore in his dream.

Then the soul of Fagir was filled with hope and triumph. "I have kept the commandments from my youth!" he exclaimed; "and shall I break them now, when my reward is so near at hand? Only one day of trial, and then I shall be walking in my radiant robe in the garden of celestial beauty, and have for companions such beings as the bright angel who left heaven to bear a message to me, the upright and the pious."

Then there came a change in the dream of Fagir: he deemed that he had risen, as was his wont, at sunrise, to go forth to the business of the day. His thoughts were not now on Paradise, nor on the message borne by the holy one; but still he wore the mysterious robe which the angel had thrown around him.

And on what were the thoughts of Fagir intent as he took his early meal before starting for the cutcherry, in which, as a government official, he worked day after day? It might have been supposed that one so pious would have reflected on holy things, when the first rays of the morning sun bade him thank God for sleep and protection during the hours of darkness. But no; the thoughts of Fagir were all on his worldly gains. He had for years set his heart on buying a piece of land which belonged to a neighbour of the name of Pir Bakhsh, feeling certain that he could derive much profit from its possession; but Pir Bakhsh had always refused to sell the ground. But Fagir thought in his dream that Pir Bakhsh had suddenly died in the night; his heir was only a child, and Fagir rejoiced in the hope that the land would now be sold, as the estate was encumbered with debt.

"The piece of ground is worth four hundred rupees[4] at least," Fagir said to himself, "and I shall manage now to buy it for two hundred rupees. I shall then contrive to make the Magistrate Sahib purchase it for a garden, as it lies so close to his bungalow;[5] and a goodly sum he shall pay! I am a less sharp fellow than I take myself to be, if, before the year is over, my two hundred rupees have not swelled into seven hundred rupees at the least."

Fagir laughed to himself at the double profit which he would make, first as purchaser, then as seller. But his mirth suddenly ceased when his glance chanced to fall on his mysterious robe.

"I thought that this garment was whiter than milk!" he exclaimed; "whence comes, then, this dull gray tint upon it?" The answer to his question came in an inscription which for a moment, and only a moment, appeared on the border,—*The love of money is the root of all evil* (1 Tim. vi. 10).

Fagir felt pained and surprised; he had often heard the Christian padre[6] say that the religion of the Lord Jesus reached even to the thoughts and desires of the heart, but he had never till this time clearly perceived that covetousness is sin in itself, even if it lead to no open violation of the laws of God or of man. As if hoping by prayer to restore his robe to its former whiteness, Fagir now prostrated himself on his carpet, and repeated a long form of prayer. His lips moved, and a murmuring sound of prayer was heard; but even while he seemed to offer supplication and praise, the mind of Fagir was still fixed on the coveted field: he was thinking how he should persuade the orphan's relatives that the ground was of little value, and how he should make the Sahib[7] regard it as worth at least seven hundred rupees. Every time that Fagir repeated the name of God—and very often did he utter the holy word in his prayer—there fell, as it were, an ink-drop upon the garment given by the angel. Suddenly Fagir perceived this, and started up from his knees.

"Can I sin even in the act of prayer?" Fagir exclaimed in dismay.

Then for an instant appeared on the border of the robe the words uttered by the Almighty Himself, amidst thunder and lightning, on Sinai,—*Thou shalt not take the name of the Lord thy God in vain; for the Lord will not hold him guiltless that taketh his name in vain* (Ex. xx. 7).

"I will think no more on this robe," said Fagir, with bitterness; "if my thoughts be tainted with imperfection, my acts at least are blameless. It is enough if a man live righteously; he is not master of his own heart." Here was at least an admission, and that from one of the proudest of men, that the heart has a root of bitterness in it that even the most righteous of mortals have no power in themselves to root up.

And now in the dream of Fagir it came to pass that, as he was about to quit his dwelling, a messenger arrived with a chit from Delhi. Fagir opened and read it, and then, turning towards his wife, he thus spake:—

"Kasiti, this note brings good tidings. Hosein, the head of my family, is coming from Delhi, and will abide for ten days in this city. We must receive him with great honour, for Hosein is a wealthy and distinguished man, much esteemed in the place where he dwells. There must be plentiful feasting here during the days of his sojourn; I will throw my doors wide open, and invite hundreds of persons from far and near to meet my kinsman."

Kasiti mildly made reply,—"Oh! my lord, your salary is but one hundred and fifty rupees; whence, then, will you spread the table for hundreds of guests?"

"I will borrow what I need," said Fagir.

"Oh! my lord," said the gentle Kasiti, "the padre hath said in my hearing, that debt is as a chain, with which no servant of God should ever be bound."

"A woman's best eloquence is silence!" exclaimed Fagir with impatience. "Bring me the pen and ink; I at once will write to the money-lender for two hundred and fifty rupees; he will send the sum without delay, for he knows that I am in government employ."

As Fagir stretched forth his hand for the pen, his glance fell on the border of his stained garment, and he read the words on it,—*Owe no man anything, but to love one another* (Rom. xiii. 8).

It seemed as if Kasiti also had read the inscription, for she ventured again to speak. "Were it not well to welcome my lord's kinsman with due honour," she said, "but with less of expense and show? We have enough to enable us to show him hospitality, not for ten days only, but for thrice ten, if your guest be content to live as we live."

"If Hosein should be content with so mean a reception, *I* should not be content!" exclaimed Fagir, his voice rising in wrath. "What! shall he who is the head of ten villages come for the first time under my roof, and find me living like a beggar? Wouldst thou have me to be dishonoured in his eyes, O thou ignorant and foolish woman? No! Hosein shall return to Delhi and report to all his neighbours that wealth and honour, much gold and many friends, are the portion of his relative Fagir!"

It was then as if a dust-storm had swept over the robe of Fagir: it darkened even as he spake; and black on the edge of the garment he beheld the inscription,—*Pride goeth before destruction, and a haughty spirit before a fall* (Prov. xvi. 18).

Vexed with himself, and all the more so because he saw tears in the eyes of Kasiti, Fagir quitted his dwelling to go, as usual, to his work at the cutcherry. The words of his wife, though slighted, rested on Fagir's memory still: "Debt is a chain with which no servant of God should ever be bound." It was a thing forbidden in the Bible! Fagir knew that there was no necessity for him to incur debt; it was pride alone, and thirst for the praise of men, which made him submit to be bound like a slave with the chain of debt.

"I shall soon cast it from me," said Fagir to himself, as he went on his way. "If I manage skilfully, perhaps I may get that piece of land for even less than two hundred rupees, for the friends of that child know no more of business than I do of weaving shawls. But I must make my bargain quickly, or Mahmud, the man who ever crosses my path like a snake, will be purchasing the land himself; I know that he has for some time had his eye upon it. He is a grasping, unscrupulous fellow, and his presence to me is as the simoom to the traveller in the desert. But lo! do I not behold him coming towards me!"

Yes, it was Mahmud himself whom Fagir beheld approaching him in his dream.

"Salám!"[8]   cried Mahmud; and Fagir respectfully returned the greeting, wishing the man whom he disliked health and all prosperity. The stain of deceit and hypocrisy was on the garment worn by Fagir.

"Have you heard of the sudden death of Pir Bakhsh?" asked Mahmud, detaining Fagir, who was about to pass on.

"I have heard of it," was the reply.

"I saw Pir Bakhsh but yesterday," Mahmud went on; "my good fortune led me to his house then, for had I gone to-day I should have found him a corpse. The poor fellow's last act before his death was to sell me that bit of land which lies close to the Magistrate Sahib's garden."

The eyes of Mahmud glittered with satisfaction as he spake; there was triumph in them, and in the smile on his lips, which seemed to the enraged Fagir to say, "I have forestalled thee and overreached thee. I know that thy heart hath been set on that piece of ground; it is now mine, and thou never shalt have it, nor so much as set thy foot upon it!"

The two men parted without words of anger, but the soul of Fagir was filled with disappointment, envy, and anger. He clenched his hand, gnashed his teeth, and, turning round, he looked after the retiring form of Mahmud with a withering glance of hatred.

"I detest that man," muttered Fagir to himself; then he started in horror, for behold red spots, as of blood, were staining his once white robe, and in blood-coloured letters on the border appeared the inscription, — *Whosoever hateth his brother is a murderer; and ye know that no murderer hath eternal life* (1 John iii. 15).

Fagir now loathed his polluted garment, and would fain have cast it from him, but he had no power to do so; that which he had received from the angel had become as a part of himself. That robe was Fagir's own boasted righteousness, and his eyes had been opened to see that his righteousness was but as *filthy rags* (Isa. lxiv. 6). But the eyes may be opened without the heart being converted; and thus it was with Fagir. The downfall of his hopes regarding the piece of ground made him but the more eager to make money in other ways, that he might indulge his pride and ostentation.

Then, in his dream, Fagir found himself seated at his desk in the cutcherry, with his piles of papers before him. Amongst them was a chit[9] from the Collector Sahib, and the contents of it were as follows: —

"There are two applicants for the office of under clerk: the one, Patras, a Christian, has been highly recommended to me; the other is Abbas, the son of a wealthy merchant. I have desired them both to call upon you, that you may examine them as to their qualifications for the office, as I have not myself time to do so thoroughly."

"Not time, indeed! the Sahib might better have said, not sufficient knowledge of the language and the people," muttered Fagir to himself, as he laid down the chit. Then calling an attendant who was outside, he said to him, "Is any one waiting to see me?"

"A young man, of the name of Patras, has been waiting your lordship's pleasure for this last half-hour," answered the man.

"Let him enter," said Fagir; and forthwith the Christian entered, and made his respectful salám.

The head-clerk had no prejudice now against Christians; on the contrary, Fagir was convinced that they held the true faith, and that if they followed the example of Him in whom they believed, they would be the most upright and holy of men. Fagir moreover knew something of Patras, and was aware that he was one who had had to bear losses for righteousness' sake. With kindliness of manner Fagir received the young man, and began, after the customary salutation, to examine him as regarded his knowledge of accounts and of other matters connected with the work of the office. The replies of Patras were all that could be desired; he was quick in answering, and made no mistakes. It was clear to the mind of Fagir that here was a man who would intelligently and faithfully fulfil the duties of the office.

Yet there was something wanting in that young man,—at least, in the judgment of the government clerk. Though every answer given to his questions was satisfactory, Fagir did not look satisfied yet. Patras had knowledge in his head and wisdom on his lips; but the young Christian had brought nothing in his hand!

"I will see Abbas also before deciding on recommending Patras to the Collector Sahib," thought Fagir. He dismissed the Christian from his presence; and, hearing from the attendant that Abbas was waiting at the entrance, Fagir gave permission that he should appear before him.

Abbas was a contrast to Patras. The face of the merchant's son expressed cunning rather than talent; his eyes avoided meeting those of Fagir; and when questioned regarding accounts, the replies of Abbas betrayed his imperfect knowledge of business. Fagir saw that the young man had little to recommend him, and was about to dismiss him, when Abbas slowly, and as it were stealthily, drew forth a heavy bag of rupees. There was no need for speaking a word; this was not the first nor the second time that Fagir—the self-righteous Fagir—had been offered a bribe, and had not declined it!

Behold, O reader! how one sin draws on another, even as do the divers links of a chain. With Fagir pride led to extravagance, extravagance to debt, debt to covetousness, covetousness to malice, meanness, and dishonour. For shameful was the readiness of Fagir, for the sake of money, to betray the confidence reposed in him by his superior, to sacrifice the interests of the public service, and to wrong a deserving man. Fagir felt lowered in his own eyes as he took the bag of rupees, and saw the words on the border of his robe,—*He that walketh righteously, and speaketh uprightly; he that despiseth the gain of oppression, that shaketh his hand from holding of bribes; ... he shall dwell on high* (Isa. xxxiii. 15, 16).

Then, in his dream, Fagir found himself standing in the presence of the collector, who wished to hear his opinion of the two candidates for the office of under clerk.

"Have you examined the two men?" inquired the English Sahib; and Fagir made reply,—

"I have done so, your honour."

"I hope that Patras is the one best suited for the situation," said the collector; "for he has been highly recommended to me as a perfectly trustworthy man."

"Patras may be a good man, Sahib," replied Fagir; "but he would make a very bad clerk. In everything connected with work, I find him far inferior to Abbas."

"Then Abbas must have the place," said the Englishman; "the public interest must ever be considered first of all."

Fagir heard not the Sahib's answer, for a feeling of horror had stolen over the soul of the guilty clerk. The robe which he wore had suddenly rent into rags as he had spoken the words of falsehood, and in letters of flame had appeared on the border,—*Lying lips are an abomination unto the Lord* (Prov. xii. 22). *All liars shall have their part in the lake which burneth with fire and brimstone* (Rev. xxi. 8).

And at that moment again Fagir beheld before him the bright angel from whom he had received the robe—that garment once so white, but now stained, ragged, and polluted! The angel spake; but the voice which had been sweeter than music now sounded more terrible than the blast of the trumpet of the archangel which shall call forth the dead from their graves.

"O Fagir!" cried the angel, "thou art summoned this moment to appear in the presence of the great King."

Then a horrible fear and dread seized upon the soul of him who had been so confident in his own righteousness—of him who had said in his blindness of heart, "I can hold my head erect before God and man." How should a poor wretch clad in loathsome rags dare to appear before Him who is of purer eyes than to behold iniquity; how should he venture into the presence of the terrible King! Fagir felt as if he would rather call on the rocks and the mountains to hide him; and, in his agony, he cried out so loudly, "God be merciful to me, a sinner!" that he awoke from his dream. And, behold, he was reclining on cushions, with his hookah beside him, the punkah swinging to and fro, and Kasiti, with her Bible still on her knees, sitting at his feet.

"My lord[10] has had troubled sleep," said the wife, raising her mild eyes from her book.

"O Kasiti!" exclaimed Fagir, still trembling from the effects of his dream; "how can a poor sinner, such as I am, weak, guilty, and full of evil, become fit to appear before God?"

Kasiti glanced down again at her Bible, and read aloud the prayer of the penitent David from the page which lay open before her,—*Purge me with hyssop, and I shall be clean; wash me, and I shall be whiter than snow. Create in me a clean heart, O God; and renew a right spirit within me* (Ps. li. 7, 10).

"Can those who have stained the garments of the soul ever renew their whiteness?" exclaimed Fagir.

Kasiti knew not how to reply to her husband in words of her own; but she turned over the leaves of her Bible till she came to the description of the blessed in heaven, and then silently pointed to the words of the angel: *These are they which have come out of great tribulation, and have washed their robes, and made them white in the blood of the Lamb* (Rev. vii. 14).

Fagir prostrated himself before the Lord in deep humility of soul. Having discovered that he was a great sinner, he now felt his need of a great Saviour. Having seen that his own righteousness was as filthy rags, he desired that his soul might be washed clean in the blood of the Lamb of God which taketh away the sin of the world. Fagir soon afterwards sought baptism; but not only the outward sign, the water upon the brow, but the inward baptism of the Holy Ghost, the Spirit which toucheth the heart.

Having received free pardon and found mercy through Christ, Fagir thenceforth manfully struggled against the world, the flesh, and the devil. He strove to put away sin—the proud heart, the covetous desire, malice, hatred, and all uncharitableness. Fagir became one who shaketh his hand from holding of bribes, and keepeth his tongue as with a bridle. All who knew him said of Fagir, "Behold one who walketh uprightly." But Fagir himself never ceased every day to utter the prayer,—*God be merciful to me, a sinner.*

II
The Church which Grew out of One Brick

I.

Gunga Ram, Ya'kub, and Isa Das were three poor ryots[11] who lived by their daily toil, and earned scarcely more than enough to supply their families with the bare necessaries of life. These men were neighbours and friends; they had heard at the same time the gospel preached by the good Pastor Ghopal; on the same day they had received baptism from his hand, and professed their faith in Christ as the Lord. Wherever one of these ryots was seen, it was certain that the other two would not be far distant. And yet, though the three were all Christians in name, toiled in the same field, and led the same kind of life, He who readeth the heart saw as much difference between them as between the diamond which shines in a rajah's diadem and the pebble which the coolie tramples under foot.

One morning Gunga Ram, Ya'kub, and Isa Das, on their way to the rice-field, passed close to the spot on which their pastor, Ghopal, by the aid of the Sahib Log, had been building a church. Money had come from praying people in England, and brick by brick the church had risen, until only the roof was wanting. Then there came heavy rains, and the river swelled and rose, and overflowed its banks. The storm beat against the unfinished building, and the labour of months was swept away in a day. The rain ceased, the river flowed again in its usual channel; but where a goodly church had been rising, alas, there were now but ruins!

Gunga Ram, Ya'kub, and Isa Das stood gazing upon these ruins, sorrowful to see the destruction wrought by the flood.

"The heart of the Padre Ghopal will be exceeding sad," said Isa Das. "It was his joy day by day to see his church rising, and to think of the time when he should gather in it his people, as a shepherd gathers his flock."

"He will build up the church again, and build it more strongly," said Ya'kub.

"Alas! my friend, where shall the money come from?" cried Isa Das. "I heard Padre Ghopal say but yesterday, with tears in his eyes, that he fears that he can get no more rupees from England. The Collector Sahib, who gave thirty gold mohurs, has gone from the station; and Manton Sahib, who fills his place, has refused to give even a pice."[12]

"Manton Sahib is very stingy!" cried Ya'kub. "He has a grand bungalow, fine carriages and horses, and feasts like a prince; he could give many gold mohurs and not miss them. Why does he not help to build up our church?"

"Manton Sahib told Padre Ghopal that the people should build one for themselves," Isa Das made reply.

Then his two companions shook their heads, and said bitter things against the Sahib who cared not to help in such a good work.

"How can we who are so poor build a church?" exclaimed Ya'kub. "We live in small huts, and seldom eat anything better than rice and fruit. I have really not enjoyed one good satisfying meal since the marriage of my younger brother, two years ago." Ya'kub sighed at the remembrance of that great feast—the rich dishes, the pastry, and the sweetmeats; for a feast was to Ya'kub the greatest of joys, and he knew not when he should taste such another again.

"If I were a rich baboo," said Gunga Ram, "I would give a thousand rupees to Pastor Ghopal for his church."

"If I were a great rajah," cried Ya'kub, "I would build a church all by myself, and make it as grand as the Taj!"[13]

"I shall never be either baboo or rajah," said Isa Das thoughtfully; "but though I am only a poor ryot, I should like to put one brick in that church;" and he looked, as he spoke, at the ruins.

"What is thy meaning?" asked his companions.

"O my brothers," replied Isa Das, "did not the Pastor Ghopal preach yesterday on the words of the Lord Jesus: *It is more blessed to give than to receive* (Acts xx. 35). When I heard him I said in my heart, 'Is that blessing kept for the rich; shall not the poor give something also?'"

"They cannot give," cried Gunga Ram, to whom his pice were dear as the drops of blood in his veins.

But Isa Das did not appear persuaded of the truth of these words. "Do you not remember," said he, "how, when the Lord Christ stood in the Temple, and saw rich men casting into the treasury of God much gold and much silver, and then a poor widow casting in two mites, He said to His disciples, 'This poor widow hath cast in more than they all' (Luke xxi. 3). The Lord accepted the offering of her who had little to give, but gave from the heart. I should like to put one brick in that church!"

And before Isa Das left the spot with his two companions, his wish had formed itself into a silent prayer. "O Lord, Thou hast said it is more blessed to give than to receive; help me to win that blessing. Thou dost love the offering of the poor; show me the way to offer something to Thee!"

II.

The three men, Gunga Ram, Ya'kub, and Isa Das, soon reached their place of labour,—a rice-field which bordered on a great river. On the other side of the broad waters they could see the bungalow to which Manton Sahib had come but the week before. It was a large well-built bungalow with white pillars, and was partly hidden by the mango-trees and the tall palm-trees which grew in the compound around it.

"See!" cried Gunga Ram, pointing towards the river; "there is some one on horseback trying to cross the waters."

"It is a stranger; he knows not the ford," said Isa Das.

"If he wish not to be carried away by the stream," observed Ya'kub, "he must turn his horse's head more to the right."

Isa Das lifted up his voice and shouted, "To the right—to the right!" Perhaps the stranger did not hear him; or hearing, paid no heed to the warning of a poor ryot.

"It is Manton Sahib himself," exclaimed Gunga Ram; "I know him by the red beard and long hair."

"He will be drowned," said Ya'kub. "See! his horse has lost his footing already, and is plunging madly into the midst of the foaming waters. The Sahib will be carried away by the current, and drowned!"

"Let us hasten to his help!" cried Isa Das; "we know the ford well, and could find it even on a starless night."

"And we can swim like ducks," added Ya'kub.

"If we save the Sahib, we shall have a great reward!" cried Gunga Ram, as he eagerly hurried after Isa Das, who had already plunged into the swollen river.

All the three men battled with the waters; all three hastened to save a drowning man; all three risked their lives to do so. The act was the same, but the motive different. Gunga Ram thought of praise and reward; Isa Das thought but of the words of the Lord—"Inasmuch as ye did it, ye did it unto me."

Before the three ryots could reach the spot where the horse had lost his footing, the commissioner was almost drowned. The rush of waters had borne him out of his saddle; only one of his feet was yet in the stirrup; the rein had escaped from his hand; he was clinging for life to the mane of the struggling horse, of which only the head could be seen above the torrent. The Sahib had scarcely even power to shout for help; but in his great need help was at hand. Ya'kub seized the rein of the horse; Gunga Ram gave his powerful aid; while Isa Das supported the half-drowned man, and assisted him to recover his seat in the saddle. With violent efforts, and with both difficulty and risk, the three ryots succeeded in bringing both the horse and his gasping rider safe back to the side of the river.

As the horse struggled up the bank, with clotted mane and streaming flanks, Manton Sahib uttered a few words which were not addressed to the ryots, and which they could not understand. Isa Das thought, and perhaps thought rightly, that the Englishman, in his own language, was thanking God for preservation from death. The Sahib shook the drops from his dripping hair; his solah topee was floating far away down the river; he had lost it in the desperate struggle for life. Manton patted the neck of his trembling horse; then turning towards the ryots, addressed them in their own tongue,—

"Brave men; you have done a good service, and shall not miss a reward. Follow me to my own house."

"As your highness commands," replied the three ryots at once.

"This is a fortunate day for us," exclaimed Gunga Ram, as the three men followed the commissioner towards his handsome bungalow; "we shall be poor ryots no longer; we shall no more have to earn our rice by the sweat of our brows."

"We will eat something better than rice," cried the feast-loving Ya'kub. "In hopes of good food, I seem already to feel myself growing fat as a baboo!" and he patted his breast.

When the commissioner reached his house, he called aloud for his bearer, and gave command that money should be brought. A bag of silver was quickly placed in the Sahib's hand; and before he dismounted from his horse, Manton drew from it three rupees, and gave one to each of the men.

The ryots made low saláms as they took the pieces of silver, and then together they turned from the commissioner's house. But the worm of discontent gnawed at the heart of Gunga Ram.

"Does the Sahib value his life but at three rupees?" he muttered. "One rupee is not worth the wetting of my waist-cloth!"

Ya'kub laughed at the disappointment of his companion. "One rupee will at least buy a right good dinner!" said he. "No work to-day for me. I will hasten off to the bazaar, and have once more such a feast as that of which I partook when my younger brother was married."

"Oh, thou man without wisdom!" cried Gunga Ram, as he tied up his piece of silver in the end of his waist-cloth; "thou wilt not surely spend all thy rupee on one meal?"

But Ya'kub was already beyond hearing of the voice of his friend. It was as if the savoury fragrance of the coming feast were drawing Ya'kub on from afar. He hastened his steps, even as the thirsty camel doth in the desert when he smelleth water, and rusheth towards the well.

"Thou wilt not spend thy money thus?" asked Gunga Ram of Isa Das.

Isa Das smiled as he made reply: "No; I will not thus spend my rupee upon feasting;" and he thought, but he spake not his thought aloud, — "The Lord hath already heard and answered my prayer. I, even I, a poor ryot, will put one brick in that church."

III.

On the evening of that same day, Padre Ghopal and the English padre, Logan by name, walked together to look upon the ruins of the native church that had been destroyed by the flood. Ghopal, with tears in his eyes, as he stood by the ruins, besought the Padre Sahib to help him in this great trouble, as he had often helped him before.

"I am sorry, very sorry, for the destruction of your church," said Logan Sahib kindly but gravely; "but I really cannot so soon again ask for subscriptions from England, and my own purse is now empty. There was a collection made for you but last year in my former parish, near London, and some of the very poorest of the school children gave to it their pence and their halfpence, instead of spending the money on sweetmeats. I heard of a blind woman who, day by day, can scarcely earn her scanty living by knitting, who yet found that she could spare something to help the Lord's work in a distant land. If she cared for the building of a church into which she never will enter, and for the conversion to God of people whom she never will see, are the members of your flock content to remain idle? Do they think it well to sit with folded hands like children, and expect to be fed by others? It is time that native Christians should learn the proverb, 'God helps those that help themselves.'"

Padre Ghopal shook his head and sighed deeply. "I have spoken to the people on this subject again and again," he replied, "but they listen as those who hear not. They are as trees that bear leaves of profession, but the fruit of good works is not seen on the boughs. Besides, my people are poor," added the native pastor.

"Was it not said of the Philippians, how their deep poverty abounded unto the riches of their liberality, for that to their power, yea, and beyond their power, they were willing of themselves?" (2 Cor. viii. 2) said Padre Logan. "Not till we see more of this spirit of liberality and self-sacrifice in the Indian Church, will God's full blessing rest upon it."

"I know it, I know it," sighed Padre Ghopal.

"And not all your people are poor," continued the English pastor. "You have amongst them baboos in government employ, who receive good salaries every month. Can you not persuade them to give at least one-tenth of their means to the Giver of all, even as every Jew did in the days of old? Shall Christians do less for their religion than did the Jews?"

"The baboos want good houses, and their wives want fine jewels," said Padre Ghopal. "If we wait to rebuild this church till the people bring free-will offerings, like Jews at Jerusalem or Christians at Philippi, we shall wait till yon river runs dry."

Even as Padre Ghopal spoke, a poor ryot drew nigh, and respectfully made his salám. "May I speak with the padre?" said he.

"He has, of course, some favour to ask," observed Padre Logan. "These people are always crying, 'Give—give!'"

Isa Das, for it was he, heard the words of the Englishman, and they were bitter to the soul of the ryot; but without looking towards him the poor man turned to his own pastor and silently held out his hand, in which there was one bright silver rupee.

"What is thy meaning? What wouldst thou have me do with this rupee?" asked Padre Ghopal in surprise as he took the money.

Isa Das pointed with his finger to the ruins and said, "I should like to put one brick into that church."

"This is strange—very strange!" exclaimed Padre Logan. "I never heard of anything like it in this country before. How can such a man, lean in body, and wearing but one garment, have a whole rupee to spare?" and he glanced with suspicion at Isa Das, for he thought to himself, — "That man must have stolen the piece of silver."

"Let not my lord have hard thoughts of his servant," said Isa Das, who understood the look. "Your servant to-day helped Gunga Ram and Ya'kub to save the life of Manton Sahib when he had missed the ford, and was nearly drowned in the river. Manton Sahib for that service gave to each of us a rupee."

"And you devote yours to the building of your church!" exclaimed Padre Logan.

"I give it to the Lord, who loved and gave Himself for me," was Isa Das's reply, as with a cheerful, happy heart he turned from the place.

Padre Logan watched the poor man as he departed, then suddenly shook Ghopal by the hand. "God forgive me for my harsh judgment!" he cried; "and God be praised that there are men in India like this poor ryot!"

A ray of pleasure and hope brightened the face of Padre Ghopal. "I will once more visit the baboos," he said, "and see if the example of this poor man will not move them to give of their abundance, even as he hath given of his poverty. But first let us together beseech the Lord to open the hearts of the people."

IV.

Was Isa Das a poorer man on account of what he had given to God? No one would have thought so, who could have seen with what a light step and happy face he returned to his home that evening. The rich flower of joy grows on the prickly shrub of self-denial; the flower blooms even in this world, but the fruit will be gathered in the next. As Isa Das passed along the dusty road which led to his hut, everything on which he looked seemed to add to his joy. There was the golden light of sunset; Isa Das beheld it, and said to himself, "Light is the gift of God." He passed where the thirsty cattle were drinking at the river, and said to himself, "Water is the gift of God." Isa Das remembered his own blessings, and said to himself,—"Eyes to see, and ears to hear, and hands to work, and feet to walk,—these also are gifts of God. The great Father in heaven loves to give. He gave His only-begotten Son, that whosoever believeth in Him should not perish, but have everlasting life (John iii. 16). God hath called us to be His children; and shall not the children be even as the Father, and also delight in giving? Yea, to give freely and to give joyfully,—this is the right of the children of God."

When Isa Das came in sight of his humble home, his little boy, his well-beloved, ran forth to meet him. The child had a flower in his hand,—a small flower which he had plucked to give to his father. Isa Das caught up the child and kissed him, and took the small flower from the little hand with a smile of acceptance, as if it had been the Koh-i-noor worn by the Queen. "My loving child,—he also is a gift from God," thought the ryot.

When Isa Das entered his humble home, he found that his wife had carefully prepared the evening meal. It was but a very simple meal, but Isa

Das blessed God before he ate it as thankfully as if he had been sitting down to a feast. Then he told his wife of all that had happened; for Isa Das was the Christian husband of a Christian woman, and they shared all each other's sorrows and joys, and nothing that the one did was ever hidden from the other. The love which Isa Das and his Lakhdili felt for each other was also the gift of God.

When the wife heard of the gift of the rupee, her eyes sparkled with pleasure, for she thought, — "My husband will perhaps buy a new chaddar for me, or bangles to put on the arms of our dear little boy;" but when Isa Das told Lakhdili that his money had gone to be, as it were, a brick in the church, she was too good a wife and too good a woman to say aught against what her husband had done.

"Oh, husband! thou hast done a good work," said Lakhdili; "and good works are the ladder by which holy men, as thou art, climb to heaven."

"Oh, woman!" cried Isa Das with earnestness, "thinkest thou that by good works we poor sinners can climb to heaven? As well might I gather a heap of date-stones together, and think by mounting on them to reach the noonday sun! Heaven is Christ's free gift; He bought it for us with His own blood. But we love Him who gave us the gift, — we love Him as my little child loves me, — and our offerings are even as this flower which my darling gathered to place in the hand of his father."

V.

Scarcely had Isa Das finished his meal, when some one approached him. The light of sunset had faded away, and Isa Das could not see the face of him who had come, but when he spoke Isa Das knew well the voice of Gunga Ram.

"Dost thou know what hath befallen our companion Ya'kub?" were the first words of Gunga Ram as he seated himself on the ground near Isa Das.

"I have not seen Ya'kub since the morning," was Isa Das's reply, "when from Manton Sahib we each received a rupee."

"Ah, poor Ya'kub!" cried Gunga Ram, but more in mirth than in sorrow. "Did I not warn him and say to him, 'Thou man without wisdom, spend not all thy money upon one meal!' His bright rupee has been to him even as a melon under which a centipede lies hidden, that bites the hand of him who gathers the fruit."

"What is thy meaning?" asked Isa Das.

"Ya'kub hurried off to the bazaar," Gunga Ram made answer; "and there, to the last pie, he spent his money on buying dainties, the fat and the sweet. And he bought bang also, and he ate to the full, and he drank to the full, till his eyes would not have distinguished the saddle of a horse from the hump of a bullock!"

"Alas, that Ya'kub should thus have cast disgrace on the Christian name!" exclaimed Isa Das with sorrow.

But Gunga Ram neither showed nor felt any regret at the fall of his weaker brother; it was to him rather a cause of mirth.

"Ya'kub became in his drunkenness as one who is mad," thus Gunga Ram went on with his story. "Ya'kub ran against the bearers of a palki,—rushing fiercely against them as the wild boar rushes through the jungle,—and, behold! in the palki was the Manton Sahib himself!" Gunga Ram laughed till his sides shook as he added, "So poor Ya'kub, of course, was sent to jail. This was the end of his feast! This was the great good which came to him from the rupee given by the Sahib!"

Then Isa Das could not help thinking of the words of the wise Solomon written in the Holy Book,—"The blessing of the Lord it maketh rich, and He addeth no sorrow with it" (Prov. x. 22). Poor Ya'kub had sought no blessing; he had cared but to gratify the lusts of the flesh; and behold sorrow and disgrace had come where he had looked for nothing but joy.

"Thou wilt not thus spend thy rupee, my friend?" he said unto Gunga Ram.

"Spend it, indeed! Why should I spend it at all?" was Gunga Ram's reply. "No; I do not lightly part with my money,—I gather it up and store it. A pice is but a little coin, but many pice make a rupee, and many rupees a gold mohur; and as the proverb saith truly,—'By patience the mulberry-leaf becomes satin.'" Gunga Ram lowered his voice and glanced round him suspiciously as he went on,—"Why should I hide a secret from thee which I have already confided to Ya'kub? The Sahib's coin lies not alone in my bag,—there are now thrice three, which I have saved by care and self-denial; and if things go well with me to the end of the year, I shall have as many rupees saved as I have fingers on these two hands;" and Gunga Ram stretched out his hands as he spoke.

"What avails our having money, if we never spend it?" asked Isa Das. "Hast thou never heard the words of the Lord: 'Lay not up for yourselves treasures upon earth, where moth and rust doth corrupt, and where thieves break through and steal; but lay up for yourselves treasures in heaven, where neither moth nor rust doth corrupt, and where thieves do not break through nor steal'?" (Matt. vi. 19, 20).

Gunga Ram gave a sign of impatience. "Preach not to me, but look to thyself!" he exclaimed. "I wot thou hast not yet parted thyself with the Sahib's rupee."

"I have parted with it," replied Isa Das with a smile.

"Hast thou then been to the bazaar and bought a ring, or a bracelet, or a new kamarband?" asked Gunga Ram.

Isa Das shook his head.

"Or a goat to give milk to thy child?"

Again Isa Das shook his head as he made reply,—"I have bought nothing, O my friend!"

"Then thou hast lost thy rupee?" cried Gunga Ram.

"I have not lost it," said Isa Das with cheerfulness.

"Thou hast not kept, nor spent, nor lost it; then hast thou been so mad as to give it away to some poor neighbour?" asked Gunga Ram, who would not so much as have given away an anna to his own brother.

"I have given it to One who is rich," replied Isa Das; and he added to himself,—"to One who for our sakes was yet content to be poor."

"If thou hast given thy good rupee to one who is rich already, thou hast indeed acted the part of a fool!—unless, indeed, he be likely to repay thee thy money with interest," said Gunga Ram.

"A hundredfold—a thousandfold," thought Isa Das, as he lifted up his eyes towards heaven. "It is there that I would lay up my treasure."

VI.

On the following evening there was a great dinner at the bungalow of Manton Sahib. All the English gentlemen of the station were invited, and amongst them came Padre Logan.

There was much talk at the dinner-table on various matters,—the last news from Europe, the state of the crops, the movements of the governor-general, and the chance of a war in Burmah. At last Padre Logan observed to Manton Sahib, to whom he sat opposite, "I hear that yesterday you had a narrow escape from drowning."

"Yes," replied Manton Sahib; "I missed the ford when attempting to cross the river, lost my seat in the saddle, and never in all my life felt myself nearer to death than I did when the waters came rushing around me, for I am unable to swim. I believe that I should not have been sitting at this table to-day, had not three ryots, capital swimmers, come to my rescue."

"And you gave each of them a rupee," observed Padre Logan.

"Unlucky rupees they were," cried the commissioner, shrugging his shoulders.

"How so?" inquired Padre Logan, whilst the rest of the company at table became silent in order to listen.

"Why, before the day was over, one of the fellows got drunk on his rupee," replied Manton Sahib. "He actually attacked my bearers with a stick when I was going home in my palki in the evening, and was so noisy and troublesome that I was obliged to send him to prison."

"But another of the ryots made a very different use of his rupee," observed Padre Logan.

"That is to say, he made no use of it at all," replied the commissioner. "But the very circumstance of his having the money brought the poor fellow to grief."

"How so?" asked Colonel Miller, an officer who sat at the end of the table.

"A rumour had been abroad," thus Manton Sahib made reply, "that week after week, and month after month, this ryot, whose name is Gunga Ram, has been saving money, pie by pie. But no one was sure of the matter, for the man's earnings were so small that it was hard to believe that he should be able to scrape any money together. But it appears that Ya'kub, in his drunkenness, had made it known throughout the bazaar that Gunga Ram, like himself, had received a present from me; and perhaps rumour had turned the one rupee into ten."

"That is likely enough," said Padre Logan.

"Be that as it may, poor Gunga Ram had to pay dearly for his love of money," said Manton Sahib. "About midnight some thieves entered his hut, and searched it, but at first could find nothing in it. Determined to reach the supposed hoard, the villains seized poor Gunga Ram, and cruelly tortured him to make him confess where he had buried his money. In his agony the poor wretch told them the place. The cries of Gunga Ram reached the ears of some of the police, who came to his aid; but before they entered the hut the thieves had made off with the money, and the police found only the miserable Gunga Ram stretched on the ground bleeding and groaning. He was carried off to the hospital at once. Thus you see that I had some cause to say that mine were unlucky rupees."

"You have told us of the fate of two of the receivers of your gift," observed the English padre; "let me now tell you something of the third ryot, and of the use which he made of his rupee, which may perhaps be to you yet more surprising."

"One of the fellows is lodged in an hospital, another in a jail," said Colonel Miller, laughing; "I suppose that the story of the third will be that he bought a rope with his rupee, and hanged himself in the next mango-grove."

Most of the rest of the company laughed; but Manton Sahib turned attentively to listen to what Padre Logan was going to say. "What did the third man do with his money?" he inquired.

"He gave it to Padre Ghopal, to help to rebuild the little native church that was thrown down by the flood," was the padre's reply.

All the company looked surprised. No one had been surprised to hear of a man getting drunk on bang, or of another being tortured and robbed; but they regarded the poor ryot's free-will offering to God as a very strange thing indeed.

"I can scarcely believe it," said Colonel Miller; and his face expressed doubt yet more than did his words.

"I was myself present when Isa Das gave his rupee into the hand of Ghopal," said the English padre.

"Then I can only say that this ryot gives me a higher opinion of the natives of India than I ever had before," observed Colonel Miller.

"You see, sir," said Logan, addressing himself to Manton Sahib, "that not all of the rupees went to the thieves or to the seller of bang."

Manton Sahib was silent for some moments, reflecting deeply. At the time of his preservation from drowning he had thanked God for saving him from death, but never till he heard of the gift of the poor ryot had he thought of bringing a thank-offering, an acknowledgment of the mercy shown to him by God. The poor man's piety kindled a feeling of piety in the breast of the wealthy Sahib, even as one torch is kindled by another.

"Are the natives, then, so anxious to have their church built?" the commissioner asked of the clergyman.

"Many wish it to be built," was Padre Logan's reply; "but Isa Das is the only one of whom I have yet heard as helping the cause by a gift."

"Then let his example be followed," cried Manton Sahib; "and my help shall not be wanting. Tell Ghopal, that whatever sum of money he may succeed in gathering from his native flock for the building of the church before Sunday next, shall be doubled by me."

"Ghopal will not gather much, I suspect," observed Colonel Miller to Manton Sahib; "your purse will not be greatly lightened."

"Whether the sum be small or great, I will keep to my promise," said the commissioner; "and the heavier the drain on my purse, the better shall I be pleased."

VII.

Before the rising of the sun on the following morning, Padre Logan was on his way to the house of Ghopal, to carry to him the news of the commissioner's promise. Before the sun had set on that day, Padre Ghopal had visited the dwelling of every native Christian in the place, and in every house had told of the poor ryot's offering, and of the rich commissioner's offer. Never had such interest and excitement been shown amongst the Christians before. The punishment of Ya'kub, the erring one, and the robbery of the money of the unfortunate Gunga Ram, were known to all; and the story of the three rupees from the lips of Padre Ghopal fell with more effect upon the ears of the hearers than ten sermons might have done. "God is great!" they exclaimed. "Happy is he upon whom rests the blessing of the Most High. Without that blessing, even money may bring but sorrow and shame."

Padre Ghopal carried with him a bag to receive the contributions of the people. When he started in the morning, there was but one rupee in the bag—that one was the offering of Isa Das; but before Ghopal returned to his home the bag had become a heavy burden, full of pice, annas, and rupees. Those who had never given before now gave with thankfulness and joy.

"I was going to spend much on the marriage festivities of my daughter," said one; "I will spend less on feasting and show, that I may have something to spare for the work of God. May the Lord Jesus grant His favour to my child; that is far better than dance or feasting could be."

"I had intended to buy a new horse," said a baboo; "but I will make my old pony carry me yet another year. I will ride him with pleasure; and mounted upon him, will go from day to day to see the house of God rising from its ruins, for I shall have put many bricks in that church."

Margam, the mother of Padre Ghopal, had no money to give; but, with a happy smile, she drew from her arm a silver bangle, and dropped it into the bag of her son. "Let the silver be changed into bricks for the house of the Lord," said the pious woman.

Before the appointed Sunday arrived, Padre Logan and Ghopal together, with thankful surprise, counted out the money which had been poured by rich and poor into the treasury of the Lord. The coppers and the silver together, and cowries also, that were found in the bag, amounted to a goodly sum; and when the last rupee had been counted, Padre Ghopal lifted up his eyes to heaven, and exclaimed, "God be praised! He hath answered our prayers even beyond our hopes. There is lying before me in these heaps half of the money required to build up our church!"

"And Manton Sahib will double the amount," said the joyful Padre Logan. "He is a man who will never flinch back from keeping his promise."

Padre Logan was right; nor had the commissioner the slightest wish to flinch back from keeping his promise. Manton Sahib rejoiced to help those who were helping themselves. Never had the Englishman written anything with more pleasure than when he dipped his pen and made out a cheque on the Bank of Bengal for the remainder of the sum required to complete the building of the church.

Fast went on the work of building; the church seemed to grow rapidly, as rice when the water rises around it. Every one in the Christian village rejoiced to see its progress, and many who could give no money gave a helping hand to the work.

"This is our own church," the people would say; "we need no more money from England. We ourselves, with the Commissioner Sahib's help, have built our house of prayer, and we will support our minister also. It is a good thing to offer freely and joyfully to the Lord. 'God loveth a cheerful giver'" (2 Cor. ix. 7).

Before the rainy season arrived the little church was built and roofed in; and there was a glad gathering of all the people to celebrate the opening of the holy house with prayer and songs of praise. Gunga Ram and Ya'kub were there; the one had left his hospital, the other had been dismissed from jail. Gunga Ram had a pale cheek, and a deep scar left by a wound; and poor Ya'kub could scarcely lift his eyes from the ground, for shame covered his face. These two poor ryots joined in the prayer, but their voices were not heard in the songs of joy.

After the meeting was over, Gunga Ram and Ya'kub joined Isa Das, who was standing a little apart, his hands clasped, his face bright with happiness, as he looked at the beautiful building standing where only ruins had been.

"Ah, my brother!" cried Gunga Ram, "this is indeed a day of rejoicing for thee. Behold God hath heard thy prayer, and hath greatly prospered thy work."

Gunga Ram spoke from the heart, for during the time of his sore sickness and pain God's Holy Spirit had spoken to his soul. Gunga Ram had resolved that out of his little earnings a tenth part should always henceforth be devoted to holy uses, the support of his pastor, and the relief of the poor. Gunga Ram would seek to lay up for himself treasure in heaven, where neither moth nor rust doth corrupt, nor thieves break through and steal.

"I am as joyous as if I were sultan of the world," said Isa Das, "when I look on that house, in which I hope that the gospel will be preached from generation to generation."

"And thou thyself hath built that church," said Gunga Ram.

"I build a church!—I, who am but a poor ryot!" exclaimed Isa Das in surprise. "Thou dost not well, O Gunga Ram, to speak words of mockery to thy friend."

"They are not words of mockery, but words of truth," replied Gunga Ram. "Without thy prayers and thy offering, that church would not have been standing there this day. It is thou who didst build that church."

"I laid but one brick," said Isa Das.

"But as from the seed springs the tree, so from that one brick laid in faith and prayer that goodly building hath risen," said Gunga Ram. "O my brother, I have learned a great lesson whilst lying wounded and in sore trouble,—a lesson which is worth more to me than the nine rupees which the robbers carried away. Our money is as seed-corn which the Lord, the great Land-owner, commits to His servants that they may sow and reap a hundredfold. Ya'kub was as one who grinds the seed-corn and eats it, and lo, his field is brown and bare when the green blade is springing up in the fields of others around him! I was as one who hides his seed-corn till the time for sowing is past, and that which might have brought forth good fruit becomes corrupted and mouldy. But thou, O Isa Das, thou hast been as one who does the bidding of his lord, and in the day of harvest greatly rejoices. For is it not written in the Word of Truth, *He that soweth to his flesh, shall of the flesh reap corruption; but he that soweth to the spirit, shall of the spirit reap life everlasting?*" (Gal. vi. 8.)

III
The Pugree[14] with a Border of Gold

It was a happy day for Hassan, the Christian moonshee,[15] when all arrangements were settled for the marriage of his daughter Fatima with Yuhanna, a highly respectable baboo,[16] who held the same faith as himself. Hassan had had a time of great trouble both before and after his baptism; old friends had turned their back upon him, and those who had often eaten his bread had crossed to the other side of the road when they saw him. Reproach had been cast upon his name, and sharp words had pierced his soul like a sword. Yet Hassan had held fast to the faith which he had embraced; he had borne losses and endured reproach, strengthened by prayer,[17] and helped by the counsels of Alton Sahib, the English friend who had first placed a Bible in the hands of his moonshee. The storm of persecution had now passed over; men ceased to revile one whom they could not but respect; Hassan earned a comfortable livelihood by teaching; and now his daughter's betrothal to the baboo whom above all others he preferred for a son-in-law, was as a crown to his prosperity.

"We will have a grand wedding, O Margam," said Hassan to his wife; "a great *tamasha*,[18] and plenty of feasting!"

"And my daughter shall have goodly garments, meet for the bride of Yuhanna,"[19] said the smiling Margam. "She shall have a shawl woven at Amritsar, and embroidery from Delhi, and slippers worked in blue and silver, such as are worn by the begum."[20]

"And what shall I have, O father?" cried little Yusuf, the youngest child of the moonshee, and dear to his heart as the light of his eyes.

"Thou at the wedding of thy sister shalt have a new pugree with a border of gold," said Hassan, bending down to kiss fondly the brow of his child.

"For the wedding festivities and the goodly garments money must be borrowed," observed Margam, who knew that the expenses to be incurred would amount to a sum much greater than her husband could earn in a year by teaching.

"Yes, I must borrow," said Hassan calmly, but with a look of thought. "To whom shall I go for the money?"

"To Nabi Bakhsh," suggested Margam.

"Not to Nabi Bakhsh, of all men!" exclaimed the moonshee; "he is an usurer who would squeeze juice out of a date-stone! Not to Sadik, for I owe him five rupees already."

"There is the English Sahib; he is a great friend of my lord," observed Margam; "surely when he hears that the money is required for a wedding-feast he will be ready to lend."

"And Alton Sahib is able to do so," cried Hassan; "his salary is five hundred rupees a month, and I doubt that he spends more than three. He has the smallest and worst bungalow in the station, and keeps fewer servants than a clerk on the railway would do. The Sahib must be laying up money; and he is so much my friend that I am sure that he would help me in this my need. To-day is a holiday in the school where I teach; my time is therefore my own, and I will go at once to the Sahib."

"And as you come back by the bazaar, O father," cried the eager little Yusuf, "be sure that you do not forget to buy for me the pretty new pugree with a border of gold."

"I will not forget it, O my child," said the moonshee with a smile, as he rose to depart.

Hassan had pleasant thoughts whilst he went on his way towards the bungalow of Alton Sahib. He considered how the Lord had brought him through all his troubles, and after the storm of adversity had given the sunshine of joy to His servant. "Those who despised me will envy me now," thought Hassan; "my daughter is to marry a good man and a prosperous man, and the grand feast which I shall prepare will show to all that this is an occasion of great joy and rejoicing."

When Hassan came in sight of the little bungalow of Alton Sahib, his thoughts flowed in another channel.

"It is strange that a government Sahib should choose to live in a place little better than a stable," said the moonshee to himself. "That bungalow is only fit for owls and rats, and will come down in the next rains. The Sahib is at home, I see, for there is the syce[21] leading away his horse from the door. Horse, did I call it! How can an English Sahib ride such a wretched tattú?[22] The tall man's feet must almost touch the ground as he rides. There is only one thing which I do not like about Alton Sahib. He is as good a Christian and as true a friend as ever trod the earth, but he must have a close fist, and be uncommonly fond of his money. I never hear of his entertaining a friend: and he seems to make his coat last for ever; I wonder whether he ever intends to buy a new one! I like a Sahib to spend freely, and never take to counting the pice. Does not the Bible say, 'Lay not up for yourselves treasures on earth'? Why does one who loves God as the Sahib does hoard up his money thus? It is a grievous fault in the Sahib."

Hassan forgot the Sahib's fault when he stood in his presence, met his kindly smile, and heard his hearty congratulations on the approaching marriage in his family. Hassan was asked to take a seat; there were but two chairs in the room, which was very poorly furnished indeed.

Alton Sahib listened smilingly to all that Hassan had to tell him about the baboo who was to become his son-in-law,—how much respected he was by all, and how much property he had in his village. But the smile passed from the Sahib's face when Hassan, after much other conversation, told the object of his visit, and asked for a loan of two hundred rupees.

"I have not the money," said the Sahib gravely; "and if I had, it would be against my conscience to lend it."

Hassan could scarcely refrain from an exclamation of surprise. He glanced round the room in which he sat, and Alton Sahib, who quickly read the minds of men, perceived that in that of the moonshee was arising the thought, "Can the Sahib be speaking the truth?"

The face of the Englishman flushed; he hesitated for several moments, as if it were a painful effort to him to utter that which he was about to say.

"Hassan, I seldom speak to any one about my private affairs," said the Sahib at last; "but I believe that it will be better both for you and for myself if I do so now. You think me close-handed and unwilling to part with my money; you may even think me insincere, and therefore a most inconsistent Christian; but I spoke but truth when I said that I had no money. The fact is"—the Sahib lowered his voice as he went on—"the fact is, that I am in debt to a friend;" and the flush on the young man's brow and cheek deepened as he uttered the words.

Hassan's surprise was now twofold; he wondered how the prudent Sahib could have got into debt, and he wondered why any one should blush to own that he had done so. There was nothing shameful to Hassan in the idea of being in debt; like many of his countrymen, he thought it a very small matter, scarcely a misfortune, and not in the least degree a disgrace. It was clear that debt was not regarded in the same light by the English Christian.

It had often been a matter of regret to Alton Sahib to see how lightly debt weighed on the consciences of many in India. He took a deep interest in the spiritual welfare of Hassan, whom he regarded as a brother in Christ. "Shall I see my brother sin, and not tell him of his error?" thought Alton Sahib. "Debt in this land is as the canker-worm in the grain, or the hidden abscess in the human frame. I can best show Hassan how I abhor it by letting him know what efforts I have myself made, and am now making, to get rid of the plague."

"I feel it due to myself to let you know something of the circumstances that involved me in the debt from which I am, and have been for years, struggling to free myself," said the young Sahib, after another pause. "When I was in Calcutta, not long after my first arrival in this country, I was robbed at a hotel of all the ready money which I possessed. This was, of course, a source of annoyance to me, but not of serious difficulty, as I had a wealthy friend in a station in Bengal, who would, I knew, at once advance whatever I required to pay my hotel-bill, and to take me up to the Punjaub, the province to which I had been appointed. I believed that the loan would be very soon repaid by my father in England."

"Your excellency's mind must have been quite at rest in the matter," observed the moonshee.

"As I dipped my pen," continued the Sahib, "to write to my friend the judge to ask for a loan of three hundred rupees, the very smallest sum that would suffice to cover needful expenses, a servant brought in letters from England. I laid down my pen and opened the first one, little guessing the heavy news which it would contain. The letter informed me that, by the failure of a bank, all my father's property, the savings of many years, had been swept away; and that he who had risen in the morning believing himself to be in affluence, had lain down at night in a state of poverty, which illness made more distressing."

"Alas! the news was heavy indeed!" exclaimed Hassan.

"My father has since been called to that happy home where there is no more trial," said Alton Sahib with a sigh; "he had laid up treasure in heaven, in that bank which never can fail. But at the time of which I speak his need was pressing; I wrote to the judge in haste, but instead of borrowing, as I had intended, three hundred rupees with the assurance that the money would be repaid in two months, I asked for the loan of five thousand rupees, to be repaid I knew not when, that I might send home help at once to my sick and afflicted father."

"And the Judge Sahib gave the money?" asked Hassan.

"At once, most generously, most readily," replied the young English Sahib; "nor do I believe that he would ever ask me for one rupee of the money again."

"All is well, then, your excellency," observed Hassan; "the Judge Sahib is rich, he needs not the money, the matter is no trouble to him."

"But it has been a sore trouble to me," cried the young Sahib quickly; "I could no more sit down quietly under that burden of debt, than I could calmly endure to wear a chain of iron around my neck. My life has been one perpetual effort to cast off that chain; link by link I have broken it away. I lived from the first on half my income—lived as no other English gentleman in my position would do. When my salary was increased, I did not increase my expenses. I have endured to be thought stingy and inhospitable, in a land where not to have the hand and the door open is esteemed a great reproach. I could not give alms or entertain guests on the money that was really another's; it was better in man's sight to be unjustly considered mean, than in the sight of God to be dishonest."

"Dishonest!" exclaimed Hassan in astonishment; the word did not seem in his mind to be in the least suited for the occasion.

"Yes, dishonest," repeated the Sahib; "money which we have borrowed is not really our own,—it belongs to the lender."

"It was his pleasure to lend it," observed Hassan.

"But not his pleasure that it should never be returned," rejoined the Sahib with animation.

Still the moonshee did not appear persuaded that there could be any harm in incurring a debt to a man who was rich enough to spare the money.

Alton Sahib rose and went up to his table, on which lay a Bible. He turned over the pages, and then silently pointed out the text,—*Owe no man anything, but to love one another* (Rom. xiii. 8).

"I knew not that such a command was in the Bible," observed the moonshee. "But the Sahib was under necessity to break it."

"Conscience does not reproach me for incurring my debt," said Alton Sahib gravely, "but conscience would give me no rest if I neglected doing my utmost to pay back what I owe. I hope, when my last month's salary comes in on Monday, to send back the last rupee to my friend; and the day on which I find myself free from debt will doubtless be one of the happiest days of my life."

"Ah! then the Sahib will be able, after all, to lend to his servant!" exclaimed Hassan with pleasure; "the marriage of my daughter will not take place for more than a month."

Alton Sahib felt vexed that all that he had said had had so little effect on the mind of the Christian moonshee. The young man closed the Bible and returned to his seat.

"Moonshee Jé," he said, "I borrowed money from pressing necessity; you would borrow without necessity."

Again surprise awoke in the breast of the moonshee. "Did I not tell your excellency," he said, "that I required money for the wedding festivities of my daughter?"[23]

"And what necessity is there that those festivities should involve you in great expense, or entangle you in debt?" said Alton Sahib. "If you could be content to put aside pride and ostentation, to place simple fare before a moderate number of guests, and avoid all waste and show, your own means would suffice for the marriage expenses. Will your daughter be more happy as a wife, because her wedding-feast has made her father act in a way that befits not a Christian? Is God's blessing on the union to be procured by disobeying God's command? What profit is there in an expensive wedding-feast?"

"It is the dastur,"[24] observed Hassan, as if that expression were a sufficient answer to all objections.

"O my friend!" exclaimed Alton Sahib, "you who condemn the worship of idols, make not for yourself an idol of dastur. It was once the dastur in England for Sahibs who received a slight affront to call out the offender to some retired spot, that the two might shoot at each other with pistols, that so the offence, however small, might be wiped out in blood."

"A very evil dastur," remarked the moonshee.

"But one so generally observed, that it was thought the deepest dishonour to break through it," said Alton Sahib. "But men were found brave and faithful enough to break through such a dastur for the sake of Christ and the gospel. It is now the dastur amongst Mohammedans to recite the praises of their prophet; it is the dastur amongst Brahmins to wear their holy threads; but you have broken through your dastur, and Brahmins, converted like yourself to the Christian religion, have cast aside their much-valued threads. Will you, O my friend, reserve *any* dastur that is contrary to the will of God? Will you say to your Heavenly King, 'Lord! I have given up for Thee the love of brethren, the favour of friends, many of the things which I prized most upon earth; but I cannot—will not—even to obey Thee, give up the dastur of half-ruining myself to have a grand wedding-feast. I at my baptism renounced "the world, the flesh, and the devil," but I reserved one thing which is of the world which I will not renounce.'"

The face of the moonshee looked troubled. His friend had pointed out sin where he had hitherto seen no sin; dishonesty in what he had never considered dishonest; shame in what he had never thought shameful. With a deep sigh he made reply: "It is not for myself that I care; but what would those of my household say if I bade them, on such an occasion, act differently from all those who dwell around them!" Before the mind of the moonshee arose the images of Margam and Fatima, and the loved child who was perhaps the dearest of all. How could he bear to disappoint them, and expose them to the taunts of their neighbours!

"Go to your family; they too are Christians," said Alton Sahib, "and, I trust, Christians not only in name. Repeat to them what I have said to you to-day. Ask them whether the pride of life which leads to sinful debt be not condemned in this verse?—'All that is in the world, the lust of the flesh, and the lust of the eyes, and the *pride of life*, is not of the Father, but is of the world. And the world passeth away, and the lust thereof; but he that doeth the will of God abideth for ever' (1 John ii. 16, 17). Ask them whether in another world, nay, even one year hence, the remembrance that a foolish dastur was given up for conscience' sake will not be sweeter than the recollection of the grandest display at a wedding? The praise of man is as the gay paper-lamps at an illumination, that last but for a night; the praise of God is as the stars in the sky, that shone ere the day of our birth, and which will shine long after our bodies have been laid in the tomb."

Hassan arose, made his salám, and took his departure. His reason was convinced, his conscience was aroused, he was almost persuaded to have a simple and inexpensive wedding; but whenever he thought of his family his resolution gave way.

"I will not return through the bazaar," said Hassan to himself rather sadly; "I should be too much tempted to buy for my darling the pugree with a border of gold!"

No sooner was the shadow of Hassan seen on the threshold of his home than little Yusuf, full of eagerness, ran forward to meet his father. The child looked to see whether the moonshee had brought anything in his hand, and the face of the little one showed disappointment when he saw that the hand was empty.

"O father!" exclaimed Yusuf, "you have forgotten my pugree!"

"I forgot it not, my son," said the moonshee, as, entering the inner apartment, he seated himself on his carpet.

"Has my lord ordered any of the things needed for the great day which is coming?" asked the smiling Margam, who was preparing the moonshee's hookah. Fatima thought of bangles[25] and ear-rings, but she was too shy to utter a word.

"I have delayed making my preparations," said the moonshee.

Margam saw that the mind of her husband was perplexed with much thought. "Has the English Sahib then given nothing?" she ventured to ask.

"The Sahib has given a great deal of good advice, but advice which we should all find it very hard to follow," replied the convert. "Be seated, O Margam and Fatima, and you shall hear what the Sahib says regarding grand marriage festivities, and the debts to which, in this country, they almost necessarily lead."

Wondering, and rather fearing what might be coming, Margam and Fatima seated themselves on the floor and listened. Little Yusuf took his favourite place close to his father, whose hand he fondled in both his own. The moonshee then repeated, almost word for word, what had passed between himself and his English friend. Margam broke in every now and then with an exclamation of surprise or displeasure; but Fatima listened in silence, with her glance bent on the ground. The large eyes of Yusuf were never taken from the face of his father; the child was eagerly drinking in all that was uttered. Though he could not understand every word, Yusuf took in the general meaning of much that was said.

When the moonshee ceased, there was a short silence in the room. Margam looked vexed, and the downcast eyes of Fatima were brimming over with tears. It would be to these women, Christians though they were, a terrible trial to break through dastur on such an occasion as that of a wedding.[26]

"I leave the decision to you all," said the moonshee, glad perhaps thus to escape from himself deciding so difficult a question. "Shall I borrow from some one else, and have all things arranged according to dastur; or shall we give up everything that is not necessary, to avoid displeasing God by incurring debt?"

Again there was a short silence. Little Yusuf was the first to break it. Clinging to his father, the child raised himself to a position high enough for his lips almost to reach his parent's ear, and then said in a whisper, — which was, however, distinct enough to be heard by all present, — "I will please the Lord Jesus by giving up my pugree bordered with gold."

The most learned discourse could not have had more effect than those simple words of the child. The vexed look on the mother's face changed to a smile; and though two big tears dropped down the cheeks of Fatima, she was able cheerfully to say, "I would rather please the Lord Jesus than have Malika Victoria's jewel, the grand Koh-i-noor!"

A few weeks afterwards, the marriage took place. Great was the surprise amongst the neighbours of Hassan at the simple arrangements made for the wedding. The feast was chiefly of fruit, the ornaments chiefly of flowers; but the fruit was sweet, and the flowers fairer than anything that man's hand could have made. Fatima was a very happy bride, for she thought to herself, "As the Lord deigned to come to the marriage at Cana, we can ask Him to be present at this simple feast, where there is nothing which my dear father is not able to pay for." And no face at the wedding looked brighter than that of little Yusuf; the snow-white pugree above that happy young face needed no border of gold!

IV
The Pink Chaddar[27]

Dear, the story of Buté, the moonshee's only daughter.

Buté had, when she was but a babe in arms, lost her mother, but she was to her father as the light of his eyes. The moonshee often went to teach a Mem Sahiba,[28] whose husband was in government employ. The Mem Sahiba was kind to little Buté; she let her sometimes come to her bungalow, and gave her sweetmeats, and once a doll from England. Those were happy days to little Buté when her father, taking her hand, led her to the white bungalow in which the Mem Sahiba dwelt.

One day the Mem Sahiba said to the moonshee: "The Sahib wishes to go on a journey into Cashmere, and to take you with him; are you willing to go for six months with the Sahib?"

The moonshee's heart was glad, for he had long wished to visit the beautiful Vale of Cashmere; but then trouble came over him like a shadow, for he thought of his little Buté.

"If I go far from hence," said he, "what will become of my only child? Behold, I have but one, and her mother is dead, and I have no sisters who would be to her as a mother. Buté, if I leave her, will be as a stray lamb that is found by the jackals."

"Have no fear for Buté," the Mem Sahiba made reply; "if it be your wish, I will place her in the school at Khushpore, for the Miss Sahiba there is my friend. Buté shall learn to read and to write, and all that is good will she learn; for the Miss Sahiba is one who fears God, and she dearly loves little children."

And thus was it arranged; the moonshee went to Cashmere with the Sahib, and little Buté was sent to the school at Khushpore.

Buté shed many tears at parting from her father, but her tears were soon dried. The Miss Sahiba looked kindly upon her, and spoke sweet words; and though Buté was shy at first, and hung down her head in silence, even before the end of the day she was as merry as the little gray striped squirrel that runs up the trees, and hides in the branches.

Buté had now many companions, and soon made friends with them all. Very fond was the little girl of talking, and in the hours of play the words from her tongue flowed on as the brook that runs down from the hills. Buté liked to speak much of the Mem Sahiba whom none of the other girls had seen, and of the grand things in her house. Buté did not take any heed to speak truth, so that the stream of her words was not pure, but as a muddy and polluted brook.

"My Mem Sahiba," the child would say, "has more shining rings on her fingers than there are leaves on that tree. The Sahib is a very great man; those who come near him bow down to the ground, and when he goes forth he rides on an elephant with a howdah of gold."[29]

Some of Buté's companions wondered when they heard her stories, and some laughed and called them *jhuth muth* (fibs); but when the Miss Sahiba heard them she never laughed, but she sighed, and her gentle face grew grave. Often, when alone in her room, the Miss Sahiba would kneel down and thus pray to the God in heaven who listens to prayer: "O Lord, show my dear children the shame and the sin of lying! Teach them Thy way of truth; make them holy, for Thou art holy!"

When Buté came to school, she wore a chaddar pink as the petals of a rose. The Miss Sahiba did not much like to see this chaddar, for those worn by all her other girls were white. But Buté did not wish to change her pink garment for a plain white one.

"I cannot leave off wearing this chaddar," she said, drawing it closer round her slight form. "My Mem Sahiba gave it to me, and she told me always to wear it."

The Miss Sahiba made no reply, but her mind was not at rest. She thought to herself,—"I never know whether Buté be speaking the truth or not. Oh that I could but trust her word! I love my little Buté—she is gentle and docile, quick at her lessons, never cross, and ready to do a kindness to any of her companions; but a pleasant child with a deceitful heart is like a fruit that looks fair to the eye, but which is all decayed and worthless within."

The Miss Sahiba used often to gather the children around her and talk with them when the hours for lessons were over; and much did they like to listen. Sometimes she told them of the dear mother whom she had left behind in England, that she might come and teach little Indian children the way to heaven.

The Miss Sahiba sat in the schoolroom on one hot summer's day, when the weather was too sultry for even her native children to go out, and they were seated on the floor around her. The Miss Sahiba felt weary and faint, for she had come from a land where the heat is never great, and the glow of India was to her almost as that of a fiery furnace. But she thought that her dear Lord had given her these children as His little lambs to feed, and she was willing to live and even to die far away from her own home, if she only might be permitted to lead these children to the Lord Jesus, the Good Shepherd, who gave His life for the sheep.

"I think that there was never a better mother than mine," said the Miss Sahiba, as she showed to the children a little picture of her dear parent which she had just received from England. "My mother was always kind and good to me, but there were three occasions in my life on which she showed the greatest love; and whenever I recall these occasions to mind, I bless God for having given me such a good mother."

The children were eager to hear more, and little Buté, who sat nearest to the feet of the Miss Sahiba, looked up into her face and said, "Tell us of these three times when the Mem Sahiba in England showed so much love."

"I will tell you," replied the Miss Sahiba; "and you shall judge on which occasion the greatest love was shown.

"The first time was when I was sick with the small-pox. Day and night my dear mother watched by my bed. If, after feverish sleep, I opened my eyes at midnight, there, close at hand, ready with the medicine or cooling drink, I ever saw my beloved mother. But for her tender care, I believe that I should have died. Was it not true love that made her watch over me thus?"

The Miss Sahiba paused, and all the children who had heard her replied, "It was very great love."

"The second occasion was this," the Miss Sahiba went on. "One evening in winter, when the fire was lighted in our sitting-room, I saw above the mantlepiece a picture that had been crookedly hung. It was rather higher than I could reach with my hand, so I brought a stool, and stood upon it, that I might set the picture straight. I knew not that my dress, as I stood, had touched the fire, until, to my great terror, I found myself all in flames! My shrieks brought my mother to my aid. She threw me down on the floor; she wrapped a thick rug around me; with her own dear hands, all scorched and blistered, she put out the fire. Never shall I forget how my mother then clasped me to her heart, and wept, and thanked God who had enabled her to save her child from a terrible death. She was herself in very great pain from her burns, but she scarcely thought of the pain."

Again the Miss Sahiba paused, and one and all of the children said, "The Mem Sahiba showed very great love."

"On the third occasion, of which I am going to tell you," said the English Sahiba, "I think that even greater love was shown, for my mother saved me from something worse than even fever or fire."

Then every child bent forward to listen, and wondering, thought in her heart, "What can be worse than fever or fire?"

"The third time when my mother showed how well she loved me," continued the Sahiba, "was—when she gave me a beating for telling a lie!"

The children were all so much astonished that they could not utter a word. They opened their black eyes wide, and stared at the Sahiba. Buté began to laugh,—it seemed so strange to her that a beating should be called a proof of great love!

"Oh! well, well do I recollect the grief of my mother when she found that her little girl had spoken an untruth!" said the Miss Sahiba. "The pain to her heart was worse, far worse, than the pain of the burns had been to her hands. She told me, with tears in her eyes, that lying lips are an abomination to the Lord, that liars will be shut out from heaven. She punished me, but not in anger; oh no, but in very great sorrow and love. Then she and I knelt down together to ask God to forgive my great sin. I could not speak because of my sobs; but I heard my mother ask God to blot out her child's sin in the blood of His dear Son, the Lord Jesus Christ, that which alone can wash away sin. My mother prayed—oh, how hard she prayed!—while the tears ran down her cheeks, that God, for the sake of the Lord Jesus Christ, would give me His Holy Spirit, to make my sinful heart clean, and to guide me into all truth. Dear children, I shall never forget that day, either the punishment or the prayer. Thanks to my mother who gave the punishment, thanks to God who heard the prayer, I believe that I have never since that time uttered a lie. Now, tell me, my dear children, did not my mother do more for me then, did she not show more true love for me on that sad day, than when she watched me through my illness, or saved my life from the flames?"[30]

Some of the girls said "Yes;" but one of them whispered softly, "It does not seem so to me."

"I will tell you why I think it," said the Miss Sahiba, who had heard the whisper. "Sin is a worse evil than fever, and the fire of God's anger worse than fire that only burns the body. It was pain to my mother to punish me; but she did not shrink from the pain, no more than she shrank from throwing me down on the floor, or scorching her own hands when she was trying to put out the flames."

Many of the girls were listening with interest and attention; but the Miss Sahiba saw but too well that Buté did not care for good counsel. The child's eyes had wandered to the picture which the Miss Sahiba still held in her hand; and while others were thinking of the lesson of truth taught by the lady, Buté only asked the trifling question, "Is the frame of that picture real gold?"

Alas! that when God's servants speak of heaven and the way to reach it, and of other solemn truths, some who might listen and learn let their attention be drawn away by the merest trifles. It is as if a person to whom a diamond is offered should turn away to chase a butterfly; or as if one fleeing from a tiger should stop to pluck a flower by the way.

It was not many days after that on which the Miss Sahiba had told her story, that her first friend, the Mem Sahiba, came to visit the school at Khushpore. It is easy to be imagined that Buté was rejoiced again to see her kind friend; and in honour of the visit, the Miss Sahiba promised all the children a feast of fruit.

The two ladies walked up the room in which the classes were assembled, and as they came near the place where Buté stood with her eyes sparkling with pleasure, the Miss Sahiba said to her friend, "Here is your little Buté, in the pink chaddar which she says that you gave her and told her to wear."

"I never gave her a chaddar of any colour," said the Mem Sahiba with a look of surprise; "what could make the silly child utter such an untruth?"

Do you think that Buté blushed and hung down her head in shame at having been found out guilty of lying? Alas! no. Buté had told so many lies in her short life that she felt no sorrow or shame for the sin. She was only vexed that the Miss Sahiba should know of her falsehood.

If Buté did not care, the Miss Sahiba cared a great deal. She thought, "Oh, how shall I cure this poor child of her terrible habit?" Then turning towards Buté, she said aloud, "Buté, I grieve to find that you have told me an untruth. I cannot let you share in our feast. Retire to the sleeping-room directly; I should not be your true friend if I passed over this matter."

Then Buté began to cry; not because of sorrow for sin, but because she had lost the feast, and was sent so early to bed. She clasped her hands, and glanced towards her former friend, the Mem Sahiba, as if to entreat her intercession; but the lady looked grave and shook her head. She knew that the punishment had been deserved, and that it would be no real kindness not to inflict it.

But still poor Buté, accustomed from her infancy to hear lies, could not but think herself hardly dealt with. Had her lie got any one into trouble, had she slandered a companion, she would have seen that sin had been committed; "But what did it signify," thought she, "whether I said truly that the chaddar had been given to me by my father; or untruly, that it had been given to me by the Mem Sahiba?" As Buté turned weeping to go to her room, the Miss Sahiba heard her murmur between her sobs, "Why does she make such a fuss? What harm could the lie do? it was such a little one!"

The feast of fruit began; plenty of nice kélas (plantains) were spread on the floor. Some of the girls were sorry for Buté, sent to remain in her bed to think over her fault; but soon even these girls forgot the poor child, who could hear from her apartment the sound of their laughter and singing. Buté lay crying, listening to the children's voices, and longing to join them.

As the Miss Sahiba, with her friend, sat watching the young people enjoying their fruit, she was suddenly startled by a scream from the neighbouring room, which was that to which Buté had been sent in disgrace. The scream expressed violent terror or pain; and the Miss Sahiba, who loved the child whom she punished, rushed into the room with such speed to see what could be the matter, that almost before the girls had time to cry, "What has happened?" the lady was at the side of her poor little charge.

Buté was standing on her bed, her face pale with terror, looking at a small black scorpion which was running across the floor. The Miss Sahiba's heel in a moment had crushed the scorpion, and in a quiet, composed manner she turned to Buté. "Why did you scream so?" she asked.

"It was on my bed—close—quite close to me! I just raised my arm, and it fell on the floor," cried Buté, who was trembling violently from the effects of the fright.

"Why did you make such a fuss?" said the Miss Sahiba, after motioning to the girls, who were crowding into the room, to leave her alone with Buté.

"How could I help making a fuss?" exclaimed the astonished Buté; "the dreadful thing might have stung me!"

"Likely enough," said the Miss Sahiba coldly, as she seated herself on the edge of the bed; "but what harm could it do?"

Buté was more and more surprised. "It was a horrid poisonous creature!" she cried.

"It was such a *little one*," said the lady, looking steadfastly into the face of the girl.

Buté did not know what to make of her teacher taking the matter so quietly; she herself was not disposed to take it quietly at all. "I wish that you would have the place searched,—oh, every corner of it!" she cried. "I should not wonder if a whole nest of scorpions were hidden in some hole in the wall!"

"That's likely enough," said the Miss Sahiba quietly; "this is a season for insects. I saw pretty fire-flies last night; I am going to look for them again in the compound."

"You think of fire-flies, when there may be scorpions in this very room!" exclaimed Buté. "The Sahiba does not seem to care for the danger to her poor little girl."

Then the manner of the lady quite altered; the cold, careless look changed to one of earnestness and love. She drew the frightened Buté close to her, held her little trembling hand in one of her own, and with the other pointed to the dead scorpion which lay on the floor.

"O my child!" she cried, "see in that poisonous reptile a type of your own sin of untruth. That scorpion could only hurt the body; but falsehood poisons the soul. Who but a fool would play with a scorpion and say, 'It is but a little one,' instead of crushing it at once! Who but a fool would amuse himself with fire-flies when poisonous reptiles were lurking near! Buté, my poor child, how many lies, more hateful than scorpions, have been suffered to nestle in your bosom and to come forth from your lips! And you think me hard and severe because I wish to crush them, because I warn you against the sin which God hates. You were grieved and disappointed at being shut out from a little feast which would soon have been over; but think what it would be to be shut out for ever from heaven, from its brightness and glory and joy! And it is written in God's holy Word, *There shall in no wise enter into it anything that defileth or maketh a lie.*"

The Miss Sahiba added many more words, and this time they fell on an attentive ear. She taught Buté how to pray for forgiveness of past sin, and for the Holy Spirit of God, through whom alone she could conquer her sin in the future. Little Buté learned a prayer before she went to sleep that night, and she thought of it the very first thing when her eyes unclosed in the morning. While Buté prayed that God would make her truthful and holy, she also tried very hard herself to be truthful and holy. Soon all her companions saw a great change in little Buté. Her face grew brighter as her heart grew more pure; for we never are so happy as when we feel that the smile of the Lord is upon us. No girl in the school was more loved and trusted than she who had once been constantly uttering falsehoods; and when she spoke of anything that had happened, however strange the tale might be, it was instantly believed. It became a common saying amongst those who knew her, "I would rather doubt my own eyes than the word of Buté."

V
The Story of Three Jewels

Dear the parable of three jewels—a Ruby, a Pearl, and a Diamond.

There lived in a country far beyond the dark waters a mighty Rajah, whose name was Kamíl Rahím (All-merciful). Though his home was so distant, he had sons who dwelt in the land of Hindostan; and the names of these sons were Mulá Mal, Bihari Lal, Tulsí Rám, and Nihál Chand.

One day the Rajah called one of his servants whose name was Narayan Das (Servant of God), and thus he gave him command:—

"Go thou to the land in which dwell my four sons, and speak to them thus: Thus saith the Father whom ye see not, but who cares for you and loves you, and desires to give treasure to you out of the abundance of his great riches. Leave the city in which you dwell, cross the river which lies to the east, and, by the path of which my servant will tell you, reach a certain mountain. There you will behold by the wayside a landmark in the shape of a Cross. Dig at the foot of it, and lo! you will find a treasure. There is a jewel which is a royal gift from myself, such as none but myself can bestow. In a setting of pure gold are three gems—a ruby, of which the name is Pardon; a pearl, of which the name is Purity; and a diamond, of which the name is Heaven. He who wears the ruby over his heart will be preserved in danger; he who wears the pearl over his heart will be kept in health; he who in the same manner wears the diamond will become the heir to a throne. All the treasures of earth are not to be weighed in the balance against these jewels, Pardon, Purity, and Heaven."

The servant Narayan Das prostrated himself before his great Master, and said, "The will of my Lord shall be obeyed." Narayan Das had a happy home, but he went forth from it; he had parents whom he loved, but he bade them farewell. The sea was wide and the waves were rough, but he feared not to cross them; lo! he had good tidings to bear to the sons of his Lord, and the joy of bearing them repaid him for all the toils and dangers of the journey before him.

After a long and stormy voyage, the messenger from the Father reached the land of Hindostan; and a few days afterwards he arrived at the city in which the four brothers dwelt, even Mulá Mal, Bihari Lal, Tulsí Rám, and Nihál Chand. Narayan Das was weary and faint, but he would not rest till he had inquired the way to the dwelling of Mulá Mal, who was the eldest of the four brothers, who lived in different quarters of the same city.

When the messenger entered the presence of Mulá Mal, he saw in him a man who had upon his brow the spot which marked a worshipper of the goddess Kalí.[31] It was the morning of a great festival, and Mulá Mal was about to set forth to bathe in the Ganges,[32] and to do puja (worship) to the idol whom he adored.

"O Mulá Mal!" cried Narayan Das, "I bring to you good tidings from your great and all-merciful Father. There is a treasure hidden for you at the foot of a Cross, and I can direct you how to find it. But you must set forth at once, or, behold! another may take the treasure, and you may lose for ever the opportunity of gaining these jewels, Pardon, Purity, and Heaven."

But Mulá Mal thought scorn of the faithful messenger, because he was not in face or garb as one of the people of Hindostan.

"Who art thou, O man of the pale cheek and red beard?" he cried; "and what dost thou ask at my hand?"[33]

"I am a servant of Kamíl Rahím, and your friend; and I come, not to take from you, but to give to you," replied Narayan Das; "yea, I have risked my life to bring to you good tidings from afar."

"I care not for thy tidings, nor do I believe thy word," cried Mulá Mal with contempt. "Why dost thou delay me, when I am about to do puja to my great goddess?"

"O my lord," cried Narayan Das earnestly, "there is no image made by the hands of man that can bestow on its worshipper Pardon, Purity, and Heaven. Wherefore will my lord not listen? Will he spurn from him the richest of treasures,—even treasures that will, if worn over the heart, preserve him in danger, keep him in health, and make him the heir to a throne? Read but this letter from your Father, and see in it the truth of all that I have spoken;" and Narayan Das drew from his bosom a book on which was inscribed these words: "The Holy Scriptures."

"Away with thy book!" cried the worshipper of Kalí; "I desire not thy jewels, nor will I listen to thee."

At that moment there was heard a loud noise of drumming and shouting; a great multitude was about to pour forth from the city to worship the idol. And with the multitude Mulá Mal went forth: he had despised the message of his Father; he had lost the treasure which had been freely offered to him,—even Pardon, Purity, and Heaven.

Narayan Das sighed deeply. "Alas!" he cried, "woe is me that the ear should be closed to the voice of friendship, and that the eye should be turned away from the gift of a Father's love! But if my message be rejected by the first brother, it may find a place in the heart of the second."

By mere inquiries Narayan Das found the house of the second son, Biharí Lal.

Biharí Lal was a more sensible man than Mulá Mal, and he did not think scorn of the messenger, nor of the message, as his brother had done.

"Surely," he said to himself, "no light cause would have made this good man leave his country, travel so great a distance, and go through so many dangers to bring good tidings to me. Perhaps in the place of which he tells me this treasure may really be hidden. Would it not be wisdom in me at least to read the letter which he says that my Father has written, and to try whether the jewels Pardon, Purity, and Heaven may not be found at the foot of the Cross?"

Narayan Das saw with joy that Biharí Lal was not as the deaf adder that will not hear the voice of the charmer. He was not as the blind man who sits hungry beneath the date-tree, and who knows not that its clusters of fruit are within his reach.

"Oh haste, my lord!" cried the messenger; "for if you delay, who knows whether you may not lose for ever the ruby, the pearl, and the diamond which are freely offered to you by your Father!"

But Biharí Lal made reply: "I cannot and I will not set forth at once, nor have I time at present even to read the letter of my Father. Bales of merchandise have just arrived from Persia; I must examine their contents. I have many friends in the city, and I have invited them all to a banquet. Business takes up my time, and what is left from business is filled up by amusement. Go your way now, O messenger! perhaps when I have nothing else to do I may seek from you guidance to the place where I may find the ruby, the pearl, and the diamond, in their setting of gold."

Thus absorbed in the business and cares of this world, the man went on his way. Alas! never, never was he to possess the treasure which he delayed to search for! On the very day on which he concluded a bargain which made him the richest merchant in the city, even on the night on which he had feasted at the house of a prince, he was smitten down by cholera. Biharí Lal died in much suffering; his body was burned, and his ashes were cast into the Ganges. Never did he find the treasures of Pardon, Purity, and Heaven! The acceptable time for Biharí Lal had passed for ever away!

Then Narayan Das found his way to the house of Tulsí Rám, who was the third of the brothers who dwelt in that city.

Tulsí Rám was a man of a pleasant countenance and of an open heart. When he heard of his Father's love, his whole face brightened; and when he saw his Father's letter, he pressed it first to his heart and then to his brow. Nay, Tulsí Rám read enough of the letter to feel sure that Narayan Das was a true messenger, and that at the foot of the Cross he was indeed sure to find the treasures of Pardon, Purity, and Heaven. Gladly did Tulsí Rám welcome the messenger who had come so far to bring good tidings, and eagerly he asked his way to the place where the jewels were buried.

"Will you accompany me thither?" asked Tulsí Rám of Narayan Das.

The messenger shook his head. "I will show you the road, but you must tread it alone," replied Narayan Das. "Fear not if you find it rough and thorny at first. Courage and perseverance are required of him who would gain the treasures; has any one ever yet conquered a kingdom by idly sleeping on a bed of roses? Go forth boldly, O Tulsí Rám! And forget not to take with you the staff of Prayer; without its help you will never overcome all the difficulties of the way."

The countenance of Tulsí Rám grew grave when he reflected on these difficulties, for he was not a man of a resolute will. It needed much perseverance on the part of Narayan Das to make Tulsí Rám so much as start on his journey, though he did not doubt the worth of the prize which he went forth to seek.

And when Tulsí Rám set forth at last, he was as one who seeth the eyes of a wild beast glaring behind every bush; he was full of cowardly fears. Tulsí Rám shrank back even from shadows; and when sharp stones wounded his feet, he first felt inclined to sit down and weep, and then to turn back and return to his home. Yet some words in his Father's letter gave a little courage to Tulsí Rám:—*I will not fail thee nor forsake thee; be strong and of a good courage* (Josh. i. 5, 6). *Know ye not that they which run in a race run all, but one receiveth the prize? So run, that ye may obtain* (1 Cor. ix. 24).

At last the traveller came to the stream which it was needful that he should cross; and the name of that stream was Baptism. The waters were bright and pure, but the banks were steep; and Tulsí Rám saw that a plant with exceedingly sharp thorns grew thickly upon those banks, and the name of the plant was Persecution.[34]

Tulsí Rám sat down on a stone on the top of the nearer bank, and wrung his hands and beat his breast, and groaned in the heaviness of his spirit.

"Oh, is there no other way than that of crossing this river of Baptism," he cried, "by which I can reach the treasures offered to me by my Father,— even the rich jewels which, worn over the heart, will bring safety to the soul, health to the soul, and the crown of eternal life? I dare not—oh, I dare not go forward! I would rather lose that which I feel to be indeed above all price, than encounter those dreadful thorns. Alas, that the thorny plant of Persecution should shut me out from the waters of Baptism!"

Then Tulsí Rám thought that he heard a voice, sweeter than the voice of an angel; and it said,—*Fear not, for I am with thee; be not dismayed, for I am thy God: I will strengthen thee; yea, I will help thee; yea, I will uphold thee with the right hand of my righteousness* (Isa. xli. 10). *Be thou faithful unto death, and I will give thee a crown of life* (Rev. ii. 10).

With fresh energy and hope Tulsí Rám arose and attempted to descend the bank in order to cross over the river; but, alas, he dropped the staff of Prayer, and did not stoop to lift it again! Without that staff he had not the strength to force his way through the thorns of Persecution. Tulsí Rám tried to press on for a time, but the thorns tore his garments and wounded his flesh. His feet were bleeding and sore, and his courage at last utterly failed him. When Tulsí Rám had gone half-way down the bank he stopped, groaned, hesitated, and then turned back. Alas, for him who had dropped the staff of Prayer! alas, for him who had lost the jewels for which he longed, because he had not the courage and perseverance to win them!

As Tulsí Rám was sadly returning to the city, he met his youngest brother, Nihál Chand. He beheld Nihál Chand hurrying on with a firm step towards the river of Baptism; he looked not to the right hand nor to the left, for his was a resolute spirit.

"How is it that thou art turning back, O Tulsí?" he cried, when he saw his brother. "I knew that thou didst start before me, but I hoped by quick walking to overtake thee, so that we might together find the priceless treasures, the glad tidings of which have been brought to thee as well as to me."

"Alas, my brother!" replied Tulsí Rám, with a deep sigh, "I turn back because of the difficulties of the road. If no thorns of Persecution grew by the river of Baptism, surely ere now I should have crossed it; but see how my flesh has been torn!"

"Pardon, Purity, and Heaven,—the ruby, the pearl, and the diamond,— are worth a little struggle and a little pain," said the resolute Nihál Chand.

"Though there were a lion in the way, he should not stay me. It is written in the Book of my Father,—*Though an host should encamp against me, my heart shall not fear.*"

"O Nihál!" cried the timid-spirited Tulsí Rám, "I am not as thou art; yet if it be my destiny to wear the jewels,[35] surely they will be mine, even though I remain on this side of the waters of Baptism. All is not in my own hands; who can oppose the decrees of Fate?"

"Deceive not thyself, nor excuse thy own sloth by talking about Fate!" exclaimed Nihál Chand. "If, when thou wert preparing thy meal, a tiger were to steal upon thee, wouldst thou quietly sit still and say,—'If it be my destiny, I shall eat this dinner;' or, 'If it be my destiny, the tiger will eat me'? No," continued Nihál Chand with much animation; "thou wouldst start up, snatch the nearest weapon, and struggle for life like a man. Even so, with courage and resolution, press on for the prize set before thee."

But Tulsí Rám only mournfully shook his head, and with a slow step and a heavy heart returned to the city.

"He is a poor, weak creature," muttered Nihál Chand, "and not worthy to wear the jewels which he has not the courage to seek. I will go forward without him."

Nihál Chand was indeed a very different man from any of his three brothers. He had more wisdom than Mulá Mal, and his acute mind saw at once the folly of bowing down to idols of wood and stone. Nihál Chand was not, like Bihárí Lal, inclined to waste precious time in delay, and to give up his whole soul to the cares of this perishing world. And Nihál Chand, unlike Tulsí Rám, had a firm and fearless spirit, and a will as strong as iron. No thorns of Persecution could stay the resolute man; he pressed through them as one who is shod with brass. And when Nihál Chand had passed the waters of Baptism, with what pleasure he looked back and smiled! Then, feeling that the worst of his trials was over, on Nihál hastened towards the hill, which was soon in sight. He could now see, at no great distance, the Cross at the foot of which the treasure lay buried which had been given to him by his Father.

On the way Nihál Chand was joined by a stranger, who appeared to be travelling in the same direction. The man was of very dark complexion, but gaily dressed, and his name was Temptation.

After the usual salutation, Temptation thus addressed Nihál Chand,—

"Brave and noble hero, the fame of your courage hath spread far and wide, and has reached the ears of your servant. I have beheld from afar with what resolution you passed through the thorns of Persecution as if they had been soft grass. Worthy are you of the priceless jewels which will so soon be in your grasp. How different are you from your superstitious and worldly brothers, and how superior to the weak and cowardly Tulsí Rám! Allow me to be your companion, that, though I never myself can possess them, I may at least have a sight of the ruby, the pearl, and the diamond, that are to the soul Pardon, Purity, and Heavenly Glory!"

Nihál Chand had at first suspected the stranger to be a thief in disguise, and had stood on his guard against him; but the honey of flattering words is sweet. The ears of Nihál Chand were so charmed by the praise that flowed from the lips of Temptation, that he now suffered him to walk by his side as if he had been a familiar friend.

Thus journeying together, the two men reached the foot of the Cross. Nihál Chand had not forgotten to take with him a spade for digging, and now with energy he set to the task of removing the earth. Temptation stood by watching him, and praising his vigour now, as he before had praised his courage.

Before Nihál Chand had laboured long, his spade struck against something hard. He stooped and lifted up from the earth a little casket of purest gold. Opening this, he beheld within the priceless jewels,—the ruby, the pearl, and the diamond,—joined together in one setting of gold.

Nihál Chand closely examined the prize. Round the ruby, in characters of surpassing fineness, were engraved the words,—*Thy sins be forgiven thee* (Matt. ix. 2). Round the pearl, Purity, appeared the inscription,—*Holiness, without which no man shall see the Lord* (Heb. xii. 14). And in delicate letters appeared round the diamond,—*It is your Father's good pleasure to give you the kingdom* (Luke xii. 32).

Temptation looked with envy and desire on the precious jewels in the hands of Nihál Chand, though not yet worn over his heart. Much did Temptation wish to rob of them the brave man who had come through such difficulties to obtain them; but Nihál Chand was courageous and strong, and Temptation knew that he had not a chance of getting the jewels by force. He therefore had recourse to cunning.

"The ornament is very beautiful," said the treacherous stranger, bending forward as if to examine it. "Grand is the blood-red ruby, and happy is he to whom free pardon for sin is given."

Nihál Chand smiled as he made reply,—"Of great value is the ruby; none but its possessor can know real peace. Blessed is he whose sins are forgiven—he who fears not the judgment of God."

"And splendid is the diamond," observed Temptation; "Heaven is indeed such a prize as the mightiest might glory in winning."

"Yes," replied the exulting Nihál Chand,—who, when he passed the waters of Baptism, had assumed the new name of Christian; "it is a glorious thing to be made an inheritor of the Kingdom of Heaven!"

"But, to my mind," observed crafty Temptation, "this pale pearl set between the ruby and the diamond rather mars the beauty of the whole ornament. The gift would be better without it."

"Yet it adds to its value," observed Nihál Chand; "is not the health of the soul a thing to be prized?"

"Your health is most perfect," said the crafty deceiver; "he who carouses at a banquet cares not to put medicine into his cup. Behold the strength of your arm and the firmness of your step! You need no health beyond what you already possess. Look again at the jewel, my lord, and say whether you would not prefer the glowing ruby Pardon, and the sparkling diamond Heaven, apart from Purity the white pearl?"

Nihál Chand looked again and again, and every time that he looked he cared less for the pearl, though this, as well as the other jewels, had been offered to him by his Father.

Temptation now drew from his bosom a paper; he opened it, and displayed to view a yellow stone, which to the eyes of Nihál Chand looked very beautiful, though, in truth, it was but a worthless bit of coloured glass.

"My heart is so drawn towards your honour," said crafty Temptation, "that I am willing to do for you what I would do for no other man. I am willing to exchange this precious yellow stone, of which the name is Pleasure, for your dull, pale pearl, Purity. I am of great experience in the art of setting stones; give but your consent, O my lord, and the exchange at once shall be made."

Nihál Chand doubted and hesitated. In his secret heart he preferred Pleasure to Purity; yet something within him whispered that it would be both foolish and wrong to part with any portion of the gift of his Father.

When Temptation saw that the Christian Nihál Chand hesitated, he knew that his own object was half gained already. Temptation turned the false stone, Pleasure, in every direction, so that the light should sparkle upon it. Again, in terms of contempt, he spoke of Purity, the pearl, as being only fit for women to wear.

At last Nihál Chand was persuaded to change the pearl for the bit of coloured glass. "Be careful," said he, "in removing the pearl, not to injure my ruby or my diamond. I care not much for Purity of heart; but Pardon for the past and Heaven for the future are possessions with which I never will part."

O foolish boast! O worse than foolish deed! Scarcely had Nihál Chand trusted his treasure into the hands of Temptation, ere the treachery of the thief was made clear. The deceiver suddenly darted down the hill, at such speed that the weary Nihál Chand, startled and surprised, had no power to follow. Very soon the deceiver, who had carried off the priceless treasure, was lost to view.

With bitter shame and grief Nihál Chand now returned on his steps, feeling like a lost and ruined man. Oh that he had had but the wisdom to know that purity of character, the health of the soul, is never to be divided from pardon of sin and the promise of heaven, so freely and lovingly offered by God, the all-merciful Father! Christ came to save us from the power as well as from the punishment of our sins.

O reader, have you understood the meaning of my parable, the lesson which is to the story even what the kernel is to the nutshell?

Ask your own heart whether you yourself resemble any one of the four men whose story you now have heard. Have you, like Mulá Mal, refused even to listen to the messenger who would bring you good tidings of pardon and peace through Christ, who came to seek and to save the lost? Will you not even read the Scriptures, to see for yourselves whether the message be true? Do you stop your ears and harden your heart when God's servant comes to tell you of pardon, purity, and heaven, freely offered to man?

Or are you, like Biharí Lal, almost persuaded that the good tidings are indeed true; and yet, are you inclined to leave the matters that concern the soul to a more convenient season? Are you setting your heart on your merchandise or any worldly gains, when Death, the black camel that kneels at every man's door, may even now, with noiseless tread, be approaching yours? Alas! remember the Saviour's solemn warning, — *What shall it profit a man if he gain the whole world and lose his own soul? or what shall a man give in exchange for his soul?*

Or are you, like Tulsí Rám, a sincere believer in the gift of God, and one who heartily desires to obtain pardon for sin, purity of heart, and heavenly bliss when this short life shall be over? And yet, do you lack courage to take the decisive step which may cause your soul to be wounded by persecution, the step which will perhaps divide you for ever from all that on earth you hold most dear? Do you think that you can keep back from Christian baptism, and yet secure the Christian's blessing? O weak and trembling believer, forget not the words of Christ the Lord,—*Whosoever shall confess Me before men, him shall the Son of man also confess before the angels of God. Blessed are they that are persecuted for righteousness' sake: for theirs is the kingdom of heaven.*

But you may be, O reader, one who has bravely passed through the waters of Baptism—you may be one who is now called by the name of Christian. At the foot of the Cross you may have found the treasure which is more precious than all besides. You may have the knowledge of the way to eternal life, you may believe in the Son of God, and you may be resting your hopes of heaven upon His finished work. But even now, oh, stand on your guard, for Temptation is near! An enemy, even Satan, is beside you, who would persuade you that every one who has been baptized is safe, even if his faith (*not living faith*) work no change in his life. The man who is willing to divide purity from pardon and heaven, will, like Nihál Chand, *lose all of the three!* He who wilfully throws away the white pearl, has lost the ruby and the diamond! For thus saith the Holy Saviour, He who is Truth, Righteousness, and Love,—*Not every one that saith unto Me, Lord, Lord, shall enter the kingdom of heaven, but he that doeth the will of my Father which is in heaven.*

O reader, may God give to you grace to take the Holy Scriptures in your right hand, and the staff of Prayer in your left. May He so guide you by His Holy Spirit, which is promised in answer to prayer, that you may fearlessly and faithfully go on your way, treading under foot the thorns that lie in your path! And may He enable you not only to find, but to hold fast to the end, and wear in your heart, the priceless treasures—even free pardon for every past sin, the promise of a heavenly crown, and that purity of life by which every true Christian must seek to glorify God!

VI
Jewels Found

A SEQUEL TO THE STORY OF THREE JEWELS.

With a very heavy heart and sorrowful countenance a man of the name of Tulsí Rám sat in his dwelling. He found no rest by night and no pleasure by day. His hookah[36] brought him no sense of repose. He cared not to go forth to visit his friends. Tulsí Rám scarcely touched the food placed before him by Juwalí his wife.

The heart of the gentle Juwalí was very closely knit to that of her husband. She was as the creeping plant which throws its tendrils round the tall tree; and as the leaves of the two are mingled together, so until now had the thoughts and hopes of Juwalí been mingled with those of Tulsí Rám. Happy the man who has such a wife as Juwalí!

The gentle woman had long watched in silence the sorrow of her husband; she had sighed when she heard him sigh, and grieved because she beheld him grieve. At last Juwalí could keep silence no longer.

"Why is my lord so sorrowful?" she said; "why has sleep fled from his eyes? and wherefore doth he put away food from him? To share the troubles of my lord, would be to me a dearer privilege than to enjoy all kinds of pleasures in an ivory palace."

Then Tulsí Rám opened his heart to his wife, for he had none other in whom he could safely confide. "Know, O Juwalí!" said he, "that some time since, from beyond the dark water, there came a messenger from my great Father, Kamíl Rahím,—that Father whom I never have seen, but who loves me with exceeding great love. This messenger, whose name is Narayan Das, brought to me and to my three brothers, Mulá Mal, Bihárí Lal, and Nihál Chand, the following message:—

"I bring to you, O brothers! good tidings from your great and merciful Father, who ever careth for His children. There is a treasure hidden for you at the foot of a Cross, even jewels of priceless value,—a ruby called Pardon, a pearl called Purity, and a diamond called Heaven. The three jewels are joined together in one setting of gold, and never must be divided one from another. He who wears these jewels over his heart will have safety in danger, perfect health, and become the heir to a glorious throne. The treasure is a free gift from your Father, and each one of you who shall seek for it in the right way shall possess it for his own."

"These are wonderful tidings indeed!" exclaimed Juwalí; "but did my lord and his brothers believe them?"

"Mulá Mal would not believe," replied Tulsí Rám; "he would not so much as listen to Narayan Das, or read the letter which the messenger had brought to him from our Father;" and Tulsí Rám, as he spoke, laid his hand on a book called the Bible, which Juwalí had often heard him reading aloud to himself. "Biharí Lal, on the contrary, believed the brave and earnest man who had left his native land, and come through trials and dangers, to bring good tidings to us. But my second brother's heart was set on his merchandise and his business, and he put off seeking for the treasure till a more convenient season."

"Alas!" cried Juwalí, "in the midst of all his cares and his pleasures, poor Biharí Lal was smitten by cholera, and he passed away from earth, even as the rain sinks in the sand and is seen no more."

"When I stood by the funeral-pile of Biharí Lal," said Tulsí Rám, "I resolved in my heart that I would not delay searching for the treasure as my poor brother had done. I girded myself and set out on my journey. Great was my desire to wear over my heart the jewels of Pardon, Purity, and Heaven."

Juwalí did not venture to ask, "And did my lord find them?"—for she saw by the anguish written on his face that Tulsí Rám had never possessed the treasure.

"But I found the journey to be one of exceeding difficulty," continued Tulsí Rám with a sigh. "To possess myself of the promised jewels, I had to cross a river called Baptism, to pass which was to break my caste; and I could not reach it without descending, with much danger and pain, a very steep bank. On this bank grows thickly that plant with exceeding sharp thorns whose name is Persecution, and briers whose names are Loss and Contempt. Juwalí, I went some steps forward; but then I stopped short, for I could not, I dared not go further! The thorns and briers had torn my garments and wounded my flesh. I groaned in the anguish of my spirit. Great as was my longing to possess Pardon, Purity, and Heaven, I could not endure the suffering through which I must pass to win them. I turned back, O wretched man that I am! I turned back;" and Tulsí Rám groaned aloud.

Tears dropped from the eyes of Juwalí. She had heard enough of the Father's letter, from the lips of her husband, to feel sure that the treasure which he had lost was one of priceless value. Juwalí had even, with great pains, learned to read a little herself from the Book which her husband prized, and she had thought much, by night and by day, over what she had heard and read.

"What makes my shame and grief all the greater," continued Tulsí Rám after a pause, "is to know that my brave and noble youngest brother, Nihál Chand, has done what I dared not do. He trampled down the thorns under his feet; he heeded not the briers of Loss and Contempt; he pressed on as a strong racer who seeth the goal near, and already heareth the shouts of those who will behold him lay his hand on the prize. He was as a hero who flincheth not in the day of battle. Nihál Chand burst through Persecution; he crossed the waters of Baptism; and now, without doubt, he is wearing the Father's gift, all his sins pardoned, his virtues shining forth in his life, and his spirit rejoicing in hope of a crown to be worn for ever and ever. I, on the contrary, a wretched coward, shall bewail my weakness to the end of my days, and shall at last perish without pardon, and sink into outer darkness."

Tulsí Rám smote his breast, for he felt as a criminal who heareth the sentence of death. Then Juwalí who sat at her husband's feet, lifted up her mild eyes and spake thus:—

"O my lord! surely it is not too late to do now what Nihál Chand has done; it is not too late to arise and go forth to seek the treasure. My lord will take yon staff of Prayer in his hand, and with it beat down some of the briers and thorns. It is far better to have the flesh torn than the heart broken; it is better to suffer for a short space than to be wretched for ever."

Tulsí Rám listened with some surprise to such brave words from the lips of a woman. Then said he, "Behold, I see *two* staffs of Prayer. Wherefore should two be provided?"

Then Juwalí blushed and drooped her head, as in a low voice she replied, "I, even I, am ready to go with my lord."

"Thou!" exclaimed the astonished husband. "Canst thou, feeble woman, endure the thorns of Persecution and the briers of Contempt? Hast thou no regard for thy caste? Thou art weak, and a stranger to the dangers of the world; thou hast ever been sheltered from all troubles, as the pearl shut closely up in its shell."

Juwalí grasped the staff, and said, though with a trembling voice,—"I am weak, but I can lean hard upon Prayer. As for troubles, will it not be a joy to share them with my dear lord? Let all my neighbours despise me, so that I be but fair in his eyes. As regards caste, surely the highest caste of all is to belong to the family of the Great King. O my lord, let us set forth at once; let us cross the river of Baptism together! I am but a woman; but I have learned from that blessed Book that the great Father loves His daughters as well as His sons; and who knows whether even for me some gift may not be reserved? Unworthy as I am even to look upon them, may not I too, possibly, receive the jewels of Pardon, Purity, and Heaven?"

Then Tulsí Rám, as from a sudden impulse, sprang to his feet. "Shall a woman be ready to leave all, and dare all, and suffer all," he exclaimed; "and shall a man shrink back like a coward! O Juwalí, light of my eyes! thy voice is like the voice of hope to thy husband. I will follow the example of my brave brother; come what may, we will cross the waters of Baptism."

Very early in the following morning, before the sun had risen, Tulsí Rám and Juwalí, each with a staff of Prayer in hand, and the husband with the Book in his bosom, started from their home and commenced their journey. The earth was glowing in the bright light of the sun before they reached the top of the bank which overlooked the river of Baptism. By this time the slender frame of Juwalí was weary; but she leaned on her staff, and looked now tenderly at the husband whose steps she followed, now on the glorious sky above her. Juwalí thought of Pardon, Purity, and Heaven, and then she forgot her weariness. Till now Tulsí Rám had walked on in front; but he stopped on the top of the bank, and let his wife come up with him. He feared that she would never have strength to pass through the terrible thorns of Persecution. Tulsí's own heart was again failing him; but when he looked sadly and anxiously at Juwalí, she met his look with a smile.

"Wilt thou not wait and rest a while?" asked the husband.

"Oh no; I am ready at once to go with my lord," replied Juwalí, so cheerfully that the soul of Tulsí Rám was filled with wonder. Beholding the courage of a woman, his own greatly revived.

Together the two began to descend the bank. Tulsí Rám was so anxious about his wife that he scarcely felt how the thorns were tearing his own flesh. Never had Juwalí been so dear to the soul of her husband as now, when, in a woman with weak frame but brave spirit, he beheld his fellow-heir of eternal life; no mere plaything or slave, but the companion of his dangers, the sharer of all his trials. Juwalí suffered even more than did her husband. After the fashion of Indian women, Juwalí wore many rings in her ears;[37] and the briers and thorns caught in these rings, so that the wearer's course was stayed, and she was as a prisoner fastened in bonds. Tears gushed from the woman's eyes. Tulsí Rám tried to lend his aid to release his wife, but only himself became more painfully entangled in the sharp thorns.

"O Juwalí! what can we do?" exclaimed Tulsí Rám.

Juwalí's answer was in her act. She lifted up her small bleeding hands, and broke off one by one the ear-rings which hindered her progress, and left them hanging upon the thorns.

"See, I am free!" she cried, smiling, as Tulsí Rám, by a desperate effort, also released himself from the briers.

"Thou art losing thy jewels, O beloved!" said the pitying husband.

"I seek better and brighter jewels," replied Juwalí. "Shall I regret these baubles if I ever possess the ruby of Pardon, the pearl of Purity, and the diamond of Heaven?"

And so the two travellers reached at last the bottom of the bank, panting, weary, pierced with thorns, but still not seriously hurt. The waters of Baptism flowed before Tulsí Rám and Juwalí. Hand-in-hand the husband and wife passed through those clear waters, the coolness of which afforded to them wondrous refreshment. Tulsí Rám had grasped the hand of his wife to help her across, but Juwalí scarcely needed his help. When they reached the opposite bank, Tulsí Rám looked at Juwalí, and lo! never before had her face shone with such heavenly beauty! It was even as the brightness of the moon when the clouds have passed away, and her silver light falls softly on earth. And never to Tulsí Rám had Juwalí's voice sounded so sweet as when she exclaimed, "O lord of my heart! the river is passed. Let us rejoice and give thanks."

The opposite bank was less steep, though still made difficult of ascent by the thorns of Persecution. But the spirit of Tulsí Rám had now acquired fresh courage. Having once crossed the river which he had dreaded, and having found in it nothing to harm him, but only refreshment, Tulsí Rám felt all his strength return. Cheerfully he lent his aid to the weary but happy Juwalí, and the two soon stood at the top of the bank, from which their glad eyes could see the Cross on the hill.

"Our treasure is yonder, and it will soon be ours!" exclaimed Tulsí Rám.

Scarcely had he uttered the words when he and his wife were startled by the sound of a terrible groan,—such a groan as is uttered only by one in mortal anguish or pain.

"Look yonder, my lord," cried Juwalí; "there is a man lying beneath yon palm-tree. Perhaps he is wounded or dying; hark to his terrible groans!"

At the sound of her voice the poor wretch half raised himself from the ground, so that Tulsí Rám could behold his face. Distorted by pain as was that face, with what surprise and distress did Tulsí Rám recognize in his features those of his brave brother, Nihál Chand.

"Can it be! Yes, surely it is my own brother," exclaimed Tulsí Rám, hastening towards the spot.

It was indeed poor Nihál Chand who, in a state of weakness and suffering, was lying under the tree. He feebly held out his arms, and was soon in the embrace of Tulsí Rám.

"What ails my brother?—he who is twice my brother—for have we not both passed through the waters of Baptism; are we not both Christians?" cried Tulsí Rám,—"though you were a Christian before me." Christian is the new name given to those who have passed through the river.

"Oh, call me not Christian!" exclaimed the miserable Nihál Chand; "I am not worthy of the name."

"What has happened; what have you done?" exclaimed Tulsí Rám with anxiety, for he saw that the anguish of his brother was great.

It was some little time before Nihál Chand was able to tell his sad story. His head drooped on his breast with shame. His brother wondered that one who had so bravely crossed the river of Baptism should now appear so weak and wretched. At last Tulsí Rám inquired, "Could my brother not find the jewels, the gift of our Father,—even the ruby, the pearl, and the diamond?"

"I found them; yes, I found them," groaned Nihál Chand, "but I never wore them over my heart, and now I have lost them for ever—for ever!" Then the stream of his grief found vent in words, and to the listening Tulsí Rám and Juwalí Nihál Chand thus poured forth the tale of his sorrow and sin:—

"I had not long passed the river of Baptism when I was joined by a stranger, dark in face, but wearing gaudy attire, and of a smooth and flattering tongue."

"Methinks I know him," said Tulsí Rám; "surely his name is Temptation."

"He walked by my side," continued Nihál Chand, "praising my courage and zeal, till my heart was lifted up with pride, and I thought that nothing but success and glory could be before me. I reached the foot of the Cross; there I found, according to the words of my Father's messenger, a precious golden casket. On opening it, I found within a beauteous ornament,—even the magnificent jewels joined together in one setting of gold. Over the ruby, Pardon, were inscribed the words, *Thy sins be forgiven thee*. Round the pearl, Purity, appeared engraved, *Holiness, without which no man shall see the Lord*. And I beheld written round the glittering diamond, *It is your Father's good pleasure to give you the kingdom.* Never was there an ornament so precious or so beautiful as this free gift from our Father."

The eyes of Juwalí sparkled at the description given by Nihál Chand. Tulsí Rám inquired, — "Why did you not at once, O my brother, place the treasure upon your heart?"

"Because of the words of Temptation, treacherous Temptation!" exclaimed the miserable Nihál Chand. "He persuaded me that though Pardon is a precious gift, and Heaven a prize that the mightiest rajah might covet, yet that the pale pearl, Purity, was what few would desire to wear. Temptation offered me in its stead a yellow stone, which he said was of greater value, and to which he gave the name of Pleasure. Woe is me! woe is me! that ever I listened to the voice of Temptation, that I ever was persuaded to part with my pearl for that which afterwards broke in my hands, as a piece of worthless glass! I thought that I could give away Purity and yet keep Pardon and Heaven. I let Temptation take my treasure into his hand, that he might separate the pearl from the ruby and diamond. But the three may never be divided. Temptation, taking advantage of my worse than folly, rushed suddenly away whither I had no power to follow him, bearing with him all that I had dared so much to win."

"Leaving nothing with you!" cried Tulsí Rám.

"Leaving remorse and shame, and a wretched imitation of a jewel, called Pleasure, which I found to be utterly worthless. Nor have you heard the end of my story. I wandered about for a while, unwilling to remain by the Cross, yet more unwilling to return to the city which I had left with such bright hopes and brave resolutions. At last I laid me down to sleep, but from that sleep I was startled by a sharp pain. The venomous reptile whose name is *Uljhánewale gunah* [38] had noiselessly crept towards me and inflicted this wound in my breast;" and raising his mantle, Nihál Chand showed a dark spot, which marked where the reptile's fang had left its deadly poison.

Tulsí Rám and Juwalí beheld the wound with grief and alarm.

"O Nihál!" exclaimed the brother, "I know too well what are the effects of the bite of the *Uljhánewale gunah.* No serpent is more to be dreaded. The remedy is at once to cut out the wounded part. This must be done, and at once." And Tulsí Rám drew forth a sharp knife which he carried in his girdle. On the handle of that knife was engraved its name — *Help from above.*

Nihál Chand was a brave man, and yet, strange to say, he shrank like a child from the pain which his brother thought it needful to inflict. "No, no!" he cried, with an impatient movement of the hand; "such sharp remedies are not required. Do not the healing leaves of Good Intentions grow abundantly in yon thicket? It will suffice to lay them upon the wound; they will soon draw all its poison away."

Tulsí Rám, distressed and anxious, took out hastily from his bosom his Father's letter, and quickly turned over the pages, to find if it gave any directions for the treatment of a case like that of his brother. Very grave was his face, and earnest his tones, as he read aloud the words of Him who is truth itself: *If thy hand offend thee, cut it off: it is better for thee to enter into life maimed, than having two hands to go into hell, into the fire that shall never be quenched: where their worm dieth not and the fire is not quenched.*

"What is the meaning of those terrible words?" inquired Nihál Chand, who trembled to hear them.

"O brother! the meaning is clear," cried Tulsí Rám. "Whatever be the anguish which it may cost, by the means of *Help from above* we must part from and cast from us whatever is tainted by the poison of sin. You can never have health, never have peace, nay, your very life is in imminent peril, unless whatever has been poisoned by the *Uljhánewale gunah* be instantly and thoroughly cut away."

Poor unhappy Nihál Chand looked like one in despair. Even the lightest touch on the poisoned place gave him pain; how could he then endure suffering which the knife would inflict?

Juwalí had taken the Book from the hand of her husband, and now, with a trembling voice, read this sentence aloud: *Let the wicked forsake his way, and the unrighteous man his thoughts, and let him return unto the Lord and He will have mercy upon him, and unto our God, for He will abundantly pardon.*

The words were words of hope, and from hope some courage came back to the heart of Nihál Chand. "I will submit," he said; "and if I suffer, I suffer but according to my deserts."

Silently but sadly Nihál Chand endured the needful anguish; the part poisoned by the serpent was cut away, while Juwalí, on her knees, wept and prayed for her erring brother.

"Now, O Nihál! you have parted with that which kept you from peace," said the faithful Tulsí Rám, whose heart had bled for the sinner even while, with *Help from above*, he had inflicted the pain; "now once more you may hope to possess our Father's gift of Pardon, Purity, and Heaven."

"Never!" groaned Nihál Chand. "When I yielded to Temptation, when I gave up my threefold treasure, it was lost to me past recovery. Go on, ye happy ones! for the treasure may still be yours; but as for me, I shall carry a scar on my breast, and a deep wound in my heart, to my grave."

Nihál Chand closed his eyes, for he was too faint and too much exhausted to speak more, far less to proceed on his way. The souls of Tulsí Rám and Juwalí were full of compassion for him who so bitterly repented having given way to Temptation, and who so mourned over the disgrace which he had brought on the name of Christian. Tulsí Rám resolved to remain for a while by his brother, till Nihál Chand should be refreshed by a little rest. Juwalí, at her husband's desire, retired to the distance of a few paces, leaving the brothers together. There Juwalí knelt down and prayed for her husband, and for herself, and for the penitent Nihál Chand. Then, being very weary, Juwalí dropped asleep at the foot of a banyan-tree.

In vain Tulsí Rám strove to give comfort and hope to his younger brother; in vain he spoke of the mercy freely offered to all who repent and cast away sin. Though the poisoned part, by means of *Help from above*, had been cut away from the breast of Nihál Chand, a painful wound yet remained, nor could he forget the past.

"Oh! that I had resisted Temptation," he cried; "oh! that I had pressed to my heart the jewels of Pardon, Purity, and Heaven; the poisonous reptile would have lost all power to injure me then."[39]

Nihál Chand was sinking deeper and deeper into despair, when Juwalí, having arisen from sleep, advanced towards the brothers with radiant joy sparkling in her eyes.

"O my lord," she exclaimed, addressing herself to her husband, "I have been sent in my sleep a strange and beautiful dream. Behold, I saw Temptation, the dark enemy, the robber of souls, hurrying away with the jewels of my lord's brother in his grasp,—even the ruby, the pearl, and the diamond joined in one setting of gold. Suddenly a white dove swooped down from the sky, and caught the jewels out of the evil one's hand, and bore them away out of sight. Then I heard a voice, sweeter than music; and these were the words which it uttered: 'Let the penitent who sorrows for sin, let the penitent who hath put away sin, again search for his forfeited treasure, and he shall find it once more, where he sought for it at first, even at the foot of the Cross."

The first gleam of hope that had appeared on the face of the wounded Nihál Chand brightened it as he listened to the account of the dream of his sister. Leaning heavily, very heavily, on a staff of Prayer, he struggled to his feet, and in a voice faint yet resolute he said,—"Let us go, and at once. If I, poor wounded sinner, must die, I will at least die at the foot of the Cross!"

Onwards the three Christians sped together. There was small difficulty to Tulsí Rám, with his knife, *Help from above*, in removing the earth which covered a golden casket. The Christian eagerly raised and opened it, and Juwalí uttered an exclamation of delight as she looked on its contents. There lay three splendid ornaments, each containing three matchless jewels, worth more than all the crowns of the world, — even the ruby of Pardon, the pearl of Purity, and the diamond of Heaven!

On his knees, and with head bowed down, as deeply feeling how unworthy he was of his Father's gift, Nihál Chand received his restored treasure, and pressed it first to his lips and then to his wounded breast. But no sooner had the jewels been placed near his heart than, to his amazement as well as delight, new health and strength were poured into his frame. Nihál Chand's wound became perfectly healed, and, springing to his feet, he again stood erect, a brave and rejoicing man; a Christian strong to wrestle against Temptation, and overcome it wherever he should meet it again.

And, like Nihál Chand, Tulsí Rám and his much loved wife, Juwalí, the faithful and meek, wore over their hearts for ever the ruby, the pearl, and the diamond, their sins all pardoned, and their lives made pure. Rejoicing in hope, patient in tribulation, continuing instant in prayer, the three Christians looked forward to the glorious time when, having been faithful unto death, they should receive the crown of life which the Lord hath promised to them that love him.

O reader! in this story have you read anything of your own? You may have crossed the waters of baptism, you may have received the name of Christian, but have you yielded to temptation, is the venom of the reptile, besetting sin, whether pride, or falsehood, or the love of money, at this moment poisoning your soul? Oh! cut away and cast the evil from you, by means of help from above, or you will surely perish in your sin. Even for your wound there is healing, even for your guilt there is pardon; the pearl of purity may yet be yours, you may yet inherit the kingdom of heaven. *The blood of Jesus Christ cleanseth from all sin*; the Holy Spirit is given in answer to prayer. But oh, delay not! for time is short, the day of grace may soon be past. It is the penitent sinner, the faithful and the persevering, who at the foot of the cross shall find the priceless treasures — the ruby, the pearl, and the diamond — Pardon, Purity and Heaven!

VII
The Broken Fence

On a high hill, in a mountainous part of the Punjaub, was built a house goodly and fair. In this dwelt a lady, whose name was Ashley Sahiba. In her heart was much love to God, and much love for poor little Indian children. Under the care of this lady were many girls; some of them were orphans, and some of them had parents who lived in the plains, and who wished their children to enjoy the cooler air of the hills. These parents were glad to have their daughters under the care of Ashley Sahiba, who would not only teach them to read and write and work, but who would also try to teach them to be gentle, obedient, and pious.[40] Ashley Sahiba prayed much with the children and for the children, and there was not one of the girls who had not a place in her heart.

But there was one of the girls who was a cause of much trouble and sorrow to the lady. The name of this girl was Ghuldasta. There were two things in her that occasioned this trouble and sorrow. The first thing was that Ghuldasta had a strange kind of blindness. She could see, and see well, every object that was but a few inches from her, so that she could read, and write, and sew,—and she did these things as well as any other girl in the school; but Ghuldasta could see nothing at even a foot's distance from her eyes. The girl never saw the path before her, and therefore often stumbled over things that lay in her way, and had many painful falls; for Ghuldasta scorned a careful walk, and never asked for a guide. Ghuldasta had a little ivory box of precious ointment which had been sent to her by her Father, and which, by his command, she always carried in her bosom. "Let my child carefully anoint her eyes with this ointment," the wise Father had said, "and she will soon see quite clearly, so that she will not so stumble and fall." Ghuldasta had the ointment always within her reach, but, strange to say, she never cared to use it at all; she contented herself with looking at the outside of the box, on the lid of which was written the name of the ointment—*Self-examination mixed with Prayer*; whilst round the edge appeared the words, *Examine yourselves, whether ye be in the faith; prove your own selves* (2 Cor. xiii. 5). Ghuldasta had heard that the ointment would make the eyes smart, and she never would put it on hers. "I can see quite well enough," she would say; "no one can read the Bible better than I; why should I trouble myself with this Self-examination? It would be of no use to me; and I dislike it of all things."

After hearing that Ghuldasta thus disobeyed her wise Father's commands, no one can be surprised at being told the second cause of Ashley Sahiba's sorrow concerning the girl. Ghuldasta was much under the power of two wicked spirits, whose names are Pride and Self-will.[41] She never saw them because of her blindness. If she could have seen them, she would have been frightened, for what is so hideous as sin? But Ghuldasta often heard their voices, and, alas! to her those voices were pleasant. Ashley Sahiba more than suspected that these wicked spirits had power over her young charge; for, though she could not actually see or hear them, she saw the effect which their company had on the unhappy Ghuldasta. Often did Ashley Sahiba warn all her children: "O my beloved ones! beware of Pride and Self-will, who often steal upon us to mislead and destroy. They are sent by the great Enemy, who wishes to ruin our souls." But though so often tenderly warned, blind and foolish Ghuldasta was not in the least afraid of listening to Pride and Self-will.

I have said that the house in which the lady and children dwelt was built on the top of a high hill. The house had pleasant grounds around it, in which the children could play. All round this enclosure was a fence made of stakes of the choicest wood. This fence was very needful, as the hill was in some parts so steep as to be dangerous, and the children might often have fallen down precipices but for this protection. On every one of the stakes was inscribed in golden letters a precious text, which glittered brightly in the sun, so that the fence was an ornament to the place, as well as a safeguard to the children. The name of the fence was Duty.

Some of the children were exceedingly glad that there was this beautiful fence around the enclosure. "There are many wild beasts in the mountains," they said; "cheetahs, and bears, and the terrible lion called Shaitán, who goeth about seeking whom he may devour. But for this fence we should never feel safe. We never wish to venture beyond it."

But Ghuldasta was not one of these children. She had always a great desire to wander beyond this fence; and often and often did Pride and Self-will urge her to do so.

Said Pride: "You have nothing to fear. What do you care for cheetahs or lions?"

Whispered Self-will: "It is very hard to be shut up in a small enclosure like this. Outside, on the mountains, are many beautiful flowers and delicious fruits. When you are close to them, you will see and enjoy them;

you will make wreaths for your hair of the flowers, you will feast at your ease on the fruits."

Then added Pride: "Could not a brave and resolute girl such as you are manage to get through the fence?"

It is very dangerous to listen to Pride and Self-will, the black serpents that speak now as the serpent spake to Eve in the Garden of Eden. Ghuldasta began to think in her heart, "Can I not contrive to break down or pull up a little bit of the fence, just enough to let me squeeze myself through the opening?" Evil thinking soon leads to evil doing.

There was one particular spot in the enclosure, shaded from view by thick bushes, to which Ghuldasta now often wandered. She never asked any of her companions to go with her thither. "I would rather," she said, "be alone." Who would have guessed what the foolish and sinful girl was doing, when she spent the greater part of her leisure time in this solitary retreat? Ghuldasta was, with a knife, day by day cutting away at two of the stakes of the beautiful fence. On one of these stakes was written: *Likewise, ye younger, submit yourselves unto the elder. Yea, all of you be subject one to another, and be clothed with humility* (1 Peter v. 5). And on the second stake was written: *Obey them that have the rule over you, and submit yourselves: for they watch for your souls, as they that must give account* (Heb. xiii. 17). Ghuldasta did not care to read the holy words inscribed on the stakes; her only anxiety was to get rid of whatever hindered her going whither Pride and Self-will made her eager to go. And, alas! all those days during which Ghuldasta was cutting and doing her utmost to destroy the holy fence, she, with the other girls, regularly read the Bible, sang hymns, and knelt down to pray. While she was obeying Pride and Self-will, and neglecting her Father's commands, every prayer and hymn from this girl's lips was in itself a grievous sin.

Very early one morning, before the rest of the girls had come forth into the grounds, Ghuldasta finished her wicked work. She had cut so very deep into each of the two stakes in the fence of Duty, that she was now able to snap them off altogether, and fling them far away down the mountain. She then tried to squeeze herself through the gap which she had made, and easily enough succeeded in doing so; for, alas! wilful sinners have no difficulty in passing beyond the fence of Duty, when once they have broken the holy commands which form it.

Ghuldasta was rejoicing in the thought that now she could wander whither she would, with none to restrain her, when suddenly she felt a firm grasp on her shoulder.

"Wretched, blind girl!" exclaimed a voice behind her, "whither are you going?" The voice was that of Ashley Sahiba.

Ghuldasta could not see the look of sorrow on the face of her guardian, any more than she could behold the love and pity in her heart; the girl only heard that the sound of the voice was angry, and felt that the grasp of the hand was a tight one.

"Wrench yourself away!" cried Self-will.

"How can she speak in so harsh a tone? How dare she call you wretched and blind?" exclaimed Pride.

Ghuldasta was not strong enough to wrench herself away; but as soon as the lady had drawn her back through the gap in the fence, the girl flung herself on the ground in a terribly sulky fit. She would scarcely listen to the lady's earnest words of warning.

"How unkind she is!" cried Self-will.

"How unjust she is!" muttered Pride.

It is sad to relate how completely these evil spirits held Ghuldasta in subjection. The girl was in a fit of ill-humour, and showed it in every way that she possibly could. She would not eat, she would not work; she behaved as if she thought that her tender friend had done her a cruel wrong in drawing her back from a perilous path. Ghuldasta was miserable herself, and tried to make all around her unhappy also. And yet this girl never looked upon herself as a grievous sinner. She had not anointed her eyes with the precious ointment contained in the ivory box.

"What shall I do?" thought Ashley Sahiba: "how shall I prevent my wilful, blind lamb from wandering in ways of destruction? She has broken down part of the fence; we cannot, with so many other children to care for, watch her night and day. I dread lest she should again attempt to escape and wander on the mountains, where there are precipices and rushing torrents, and where wild beasts roam about seeking for prey."

After anxious thought Ashley Sahiba had the gap in the fence filled up by a quantity of sharp prickly thorns of which the name is Punishment. "Now I trust that my child will be safe," thought she.

On the first opportunity the wilful Ghuldasta found her way back to the spot where she had broken a way through the fence; but when she attempted to pass through the gap, lo! sharp Punishment stayed her.

"Cruel, cruel Mem Sahiba!" exclaimed Ghuldasta, as she drew back her bleeding hand, which had been hurt by the thorns.

"She shall never stop you in this way!" cried Self-will.

"She finds fault with you because she does not love you as she loves the other girls," muttered Pride. "She is hard, partial, and unjust."

Ghuldasta resolved that even Punishment should not stop her. She remained all the rest of that day sulky and silent, revolving in her mind by what means she could still get her own way. Even during prayer-time all the thoughts of the sinful girl were turned in this direction. While the Mem Sahiba was reading the Bible aloud to her children, Ghuldasta was listening to the whispers of Pride and Self-will, which none could hear but herself.

Said Pride: "When none are near to watch you, take the thick black rug of Obstinacy and throw it right over the thorns. They may hurt you a little still, but they will not be able to stay you."

"You will not care for a little pain, so that you get your own way," cried Self-will.

When the house was hushed in silence,—when all the other girls were sleeping, and the weary Ashley Sahiba had closed her eyes in repose,— Ghuldasta silently arose from her bed, and felt her way to the place where hung the black rug. Bearing Obstinacy with her, and moving as stealthily as if she were a thief, the wilful girl contrived to quit the house and reach the spot to which she so often had turned her steps before. Ghuldasta flung the rug of Obstinacy over the thorns of Punishment, and found that by means of it she could manage to clamber over, though not without some pain. Ghuldasta was so much delighted at this, that almost unconsciously she began to sing, though in a tone too low to rouse any of the sleepers in the house, which was at some distance. Ghuldasta—O fearful mockery!—was actually humming a hymn when she passed beyond the fence of Duty. She had on her lips:

"There is a happy land,

Far, far away."[42]

But she was not to have time to sing about the "saints," whose glory, if she went on in her wilful course, she never, never would share. Ghuldasta, though she knew it not, was on the path that leadeth to destruction. She had no right to sing of that happy land, from which she was actually trying to shut herself out for ever.

I have said that Ghuldasta was apt to walk carelessly, and that she was so near-sighted that, even in the light of day, she could not see the path before her. Suddenly, to her horror, the poor girl found herself plunging down a precipice! Screaming for help, Ghuldasta caught at the bushes to save herself: they somewhat broke but they could not prevent her fall; for the twigs gave way in her hand! Down—down—down,—crashing fell the miserable child! What would she not have given to have felt the firm grasp of her Mem Sahiba! what would she not have given to have been held fast by the thorns of Punishment!—anything, anything that might have saved her from the consequences of her own blind folly!

Poor Ghuldasta was senseless before she reached the bottom. Her clothes were rent; her body bruised and bleeding; much of her hair had been left on the bushes. After a while she came to herself, in terrible pain, and with perfect darkness around her. As Ghuldasta could only see objects very, very near her, it was now to her as if she lay at the bottom of a well.

"Where am I?" faintly murmured the miserable girl. Gradually she remembered all that had happened; but memory was anguish. Her best friend, her much-wronged friend, was, she doubted not, sleeping, all unconscious of the misery and danger of the ungrateful girl whom she had warned in vain. Ghuldasta's young companions were slumbering in peace, till the morning's light should awaken them to begin the occupations of the day. But for her own pride and wilfulness, Ghuldasta might at that moment have been safe and happy amongst them.

Ghuldasta longed to know where she was—to be able to look around her. She thought of her ivory box of ointment, which she still carried in her bosom. Ghuldasta could not move her arm without pain, and she knew well that the ointment would make her eyes smart; but lying as she was in helplessness and darkness in a strange place, for the first time the girl wished to obey her Father's command.

Ghuldasta anointed her eyes with the salve of *Self-examination mixed with Prayer,* and the effect of that salve was marvellous beyond all expectation. At once perfect sight appeared to be restored; Ghuldasta saw everything around her bathed in the light of a clear full moon.

But it was a terrible view that was presented to the wilful transgressor. She saw her danger—she saw her sin. Above her was a rude jagged cliff, which, even had she been unhurt by her fall, she could never have power to climb. Ghuldasta lay upon thorns more painful than the thorns of Punishment which she had thought so cruel, and from these thorns she could not wrench herself free.

"Oh! what shall I do!—what shall I do!" exclaimed the unhappy and penitent girl, after she had exhausted herself by cries for help which no one could hear. "Would that I had never listened to the voices of the tempters!— would that I had never broken through the fence of Duty, and left my safe and happy home! I chose my own way; and a way of misery I have found it. I was lifted up with pride, and now I have fallen into the depths of despair!"

Ghuldasta could distinguish objects lying at no great distance from her, which she at once recognized; for on them golden letters were faintly glimmering in the moonlight. These were the stakes from the fence of Duty which she had herself broken and flung away!

"*Likewise, ye younger, submit yourselves unto the elder,*" faintly murmured Ghuldasta, as tears flowed fast down her cheeks. "Alas! *I* would never submit; I was never clothed in humility; I would not obey her whom my Father had placed over me; I was insolent to her in my manner, I despised her wise commands, I abused her patience, I grieved her heart. I shall never, never see her again. Oh! will she ever give a sorrowful thought to her poor Ghuldasta! No, no; she will be happy with those who love her — those who obey her. I shall soon be forgotten by all. Even in heaven they will never meet, nor even miss, the wretched Ghuldasta!" At the miserable thought, the poor girl cried as if her heart would break.

Hark! what was that fearful sound in the distance? Was it not the roar of the lion who goeth about seeking whom he may devour? Ghuldasta could not fight, and she could not flee. She was ready to faint with terror. Then in her agony the repentant sinner betook herself to prayer. Never, never had poor Ghuldasta prayed before as she prayed on that night, with clasped hands and streaming eyes! Her supplications were no mockery now — they came from a broken and contrite heart.

Ashley Sahiba, meanwhile, lay asleep on her bed; but even in sleep her mind was restless. Thoughts of her self-willed, proud Ghuldasta mixed themselves with her dreams. At last the lady suddenly awoke, for it seemed as if a voice were whispering in her ears: "O shepherdess! where is your poor lost lamb?"

Ashley Sahiba closed her tired eyes, and tried to go to sleep again, but she could not; she was so unhappy about Ghuldasta. Presently she arose, and knelt down and prayed for the child. Then softly moving along the rows of beds on which the children were sleeping, the lady sought that of Ghuldasta, and started to find it empty! Her fears were but too well-founded — Ghuldasta had fled! That moment was one of the most painful which the lady had ever known in the course of her life.

Ghuldasta, imprisoned by thorns, and sorely hurt by her fall, lay straining her eyes to catch sounds in the distance, and exhausted her little remaining strength by weeping. At last, to her exceeding terror, she saw the bushes on the cliff above her moving, as if some large animal were forcing its way down the difficult descent. She expected every moment to see the glaring eyes of a beast of prey; she became silent in the extremity of her fear. Then, from the very spot from whence Ghuldasta expected to hear a savage growl, came a dear and well-known voice: "My child! my child! where are you?" Ghuldasta, collecting all her strength, called out the name of her lady; and a glad voice answered from above. Heedless of weariness or danger, Ashley Sahiba, by help of the bushes, was clambering down the cliff from the top of which Ghuldasta had fallen. The lady was like the good shepherd seeking the straying sheep; like the woman searching for the lost piece of silver; and when at last she clasped her Ghuldasta in her arms, her cry of joy was like that of the prodigal's father: *This my son was dead and is alive again; was lost, and is found.*

Ashley Sahiba was followed by servants whom she had roused to help in the search for Ghuldasta, and who had made their way down the hill by a longer but less dangerous path. The poor girl, clinging to her Mem Sahiba, was raised from her painful position, and carried up on a litter, for she was unable to walk.

A fever succeeded, caused by the sufferings both of mind and body endured on that night by Ghuldasta. Under careful nursing she recovered from the fever, but the poor girl carried on her to her dying day marks of her terrible fall, and the remembrance of it was never effaced from her mind. But happy was it for Ghuldasta that she had learned to anoint her eyes with the salve of *Self-examination mixed with Prayer*; happy was it for her that she could say, *Whereas I was blind, now I see.* Ghuldasta had parted company with Pride and Self-will; she became daily more meek and lowly, more like Him who, though God as well as man, deigned in His youth to be subject to a mortal mother. Ghuldasta became the joy and crown of the faithful friend to whom she so long had been a cause of trouble and sorrow. That friend taught her where alone she could find forgiveness for all her past sins, and grace to struggle against them in the future. *Blessed are they that mourn: for they shall be comforted. Blessed are the poor in spirit: for theirs is the kingdom of heaven* (Matt. v. 4, 3).

VIII
Shining in the Dark

There dwelt in the Punjaub a man of the name of Bál Mukand, who was very learned and clever. He had read many hooks, Hindu, Sanscrit, and Arabic, the Vedas and the Puránas; he had also read translations of many of the writings of the English.

Bál Mukand entered the shop of Shib Das, the goldsmith, and sat down beside him. Shib Das had lost many friends because he had become a Christian, but he had not lost the friendship of Bál Mukand. "I will not quarrel with a man because he wears not on his head a pugree (turban) of the same colour as mine, or because he has not the same thoughts in his head as I have," said the liberal-minded Punjaubi. He had read and reflected too much to act the part of a bigot.

And what were the thoughts of Bál Mukand on the subject of religion? Thus he expressed them to Shib Das as he sat in his shop.

"I will never be a Christian!" said he. "Excepting yourself, O Shib Das, I think that of all people Christians are the worst."

"And why do you think so?" inquired Shib Das.

"I have read the Koran and the Shastras, I have read the Vedas and the Bible," replied Bál Mukand, "and I compare the books with the people who severally profess to make such various writings the rule of their faith. The Mohammedan is commanded to fast in the Ramadan, and he fasts; he is commanded to pray five times a day, and he prays. The Hindu is told to reverence the Brahman; and lo! he is ready to drink the water in which the holy man's feet have been washed. The Hindu makes pilgrimages and visits temples, performs ablutions, and will rather starve than eat that which he deems unclean."

"True, O Bál Mukand," replied Shib Das; "but why call Christians the worst of men? If they make not pilgrimages nor observe long fasts, it is because their religion does not command them to do these things."

"But their religion does command them to do many things which they do not," exclaimed Bál Mukand with a sneer. "I have read their Bible, and know what is in it, and very good words they are. The Bible says, *Love one another*; and how many Christians hate one another instead! The Bible says, *Thou shalt not covet*; and where is the Christian who is not greedy of gain? The Christians read in their Book that God is truth, they call themselves His children; and yet how many tell lies! The Mohammedan obeys his Koran, and the Hindu follows the rules of his Vedas; but the Christian reads his holy Book, and obeys not. When his guide bids him take the narrow path, he rushes off to the broad one. Therefore, I repeat again, Christians are the worst of all men."[43]

"You are somewhat unjust to them," observed Shib Das. "Not all Christians act in the manner which you describe."

"Look at the Sahib log" (English), exclaimed Bál Mukand; "they who think that they walk in light, while all the rest of mankind lie in darkness! See the Commissioner Sahib—has he not read in his Book, *Be pitiful, be courteous*; and yet he spurns natives from him as if they were no better than dogs! Who is more fond of the world and of money than the Railway Sahib; and look how some of the English soldiers drink, though it is written in their Bible that drunkards shall not inherit the kingdom of heaven! Their religion may be pure as rain from the sky, or stream from the mountain, but wherein are they the better for it?"

Then Shib Das thoughtfully stroked his beard and made reply: "If fruit grow not on the stone, is it the fault of the rain? if the traveller stoop not to drink of the stream beside him, is it the fault of the river if he perish of thirst? I repeat again that all Christians are not so disobedient to the laws of their Book; there are some whose souls are as a well-watered garden, in which grow the fruits of holiness, truth, and love."

"These people are very few," muttered Bál Mukand; "I could count on my fingers all whom I have met with. As by far the greater number of Christians are evil, where is the advantage of becoming a Christian?"

Shib Das smiled and said: "O Bál Mukand, did you ever hear the tradition of King Solomon and the Queen of Sheba?"

Then said Bál Mukand, "I pray you tell me the story."

"It is said that the Queen of Sheba, who came from afar to hear the wisdom of Solomon, tried thus to put it to proof. She had flowers made by skilful workmen so like real flowers, that no man, without touching them, could tell the difference between them. The queen showed to Solomon a quantity of true and false flowers mixed together. 'Let your wisdom,' said she, 'discover, without coming near them, which of the flowers have drank heaven's dews and which have not,—which are living and which are lifeless.'"

"And what did the wise Solomon?" inquired Bál Mukand.

"He commanded all the doors to be flung wide open, so that the bees and other insects had free access to the flowers. The bees settled on the blossoms that had life, those in which heaven's dew had turned into honey. 'Behold, O Queen,' cried Solomon, 'where there is life there is sweetness also. There are many false flowers yonder, but we soon discover the true.' Even so, O Bál Mukand, there are many that are called Christians who are not Christians at all, for in their faith there is no life; they have nothing of Christianity but the name. Would Solomon have been a wise man had he said at once, 'All these flowers are false'? No; he put the matter to the proof. When you condemn all Christians together, you have not the wisdom of Solomon nor the discrimination of the bees. Besides," added Shib Das, "whatever the conduct of so-called Christians may be, you acknowledge that their religion is pure, that their Book is good. Christians may be faulty, but Christ Himself is perfect."

"One looks for the disciples to be as the Master," observed Bál Mukand. "The Christian's heaven may exist, and be all that the Bible describes it to be; but to me the path to it is so dark, that after all my reading, and searching, and thinking, I own that I cannot find it. I never shall be a Christian."

Shib Das saw that there was no use in arguing with one who refused to be convinced; therefore the Christian remained silent. And soon afterwards Bál Mukand fell asleep.

Bál Mukand was before long awakened by the sound of some one speaking at the front of the shop, but he stirred not, nor opened his eyes; he remained as if sleeping still, and listened unnoticed to the discourse of Shib Das with the stranger, whose name was Karm Illahi.

There was in the shop a scimitar with a jewelled hilt, which had attracted the eyes of Karm Illahi as he passed along the narrow street. At his desire it was now placed in his hand; he examined the blade, he looked at the ornaments on the hilt. Bál Mukand also had, half an hour before, noticed and admired the scimitar, which had been, a short time previously, purchased by Shib Das from an Afghan chief.

The Mohammedan, Karm Illahi, inquired the price of the scimitar, which he greatly desired to possess.

"The price is thirty rupees," was the reply of Shib Das.

"I thought that he would have said sixty or seventy at least," thought the astonished Bál Mukand. "Surely the jewels in the hilt are worth much more than thirty rupees."

Karm Illahi did not betray the joy which he really felt at hearing a much lower price asked than what he had expected. Again, slowly and carefully, he tried the blade and examined the hilt.

"Are all these jewels real?" he inquired of the seller.

"All but this sapphire in the centre," replied Shib Das. "The imitation is so good that I myself was at first deceived. Were that jewel real, I should have asked double the price for the weapon."

"I will give you twenty rupees," said Karm Illahi—who had never yet bought anything without trying to lower the price. Had he been offered a hen for an anna, he would have tried to get it for eleven pies.[44]

"No," replied Shib Das calmly; "I have but one price for the things in my shop, and that is the fair one. A year ago I should have asked you at least seventy rupees for that scimitar, and have sworn that every jewel in the hilt was real."

"And why do you not do so now?" inquired Karm Illahi in no small surprise.

"Because I am a Christian," was the simple reply of Shib Das.

Karm Illahi smiled a mocking smile, but he drew forth a bag of money which he carried with him, and counted out the thirty rupees. Bál Mukand heard him muttering to himself as he did so: "This Christian is a fool, for none but a fool would have said that the stone was false, or have asked less for his goods than he might have hoped to get from a stranger."

Not such was the thought of the more enlightened Bál Mukand. "If all men dealt with such honesty and truth, this would be a happy land," he said in his heart. "The folly of such men as this Shib Das is better than the wisdom of the worldly."

Scarcely had the Mussulman left the place with the scimitar which he had bought, than Yuhanna, a Christian catechist, came up to the jeweller's shop. Still Bál Mukand lay perfectly quiet and listened, whilst Yuhanna exchanged greetings with Shib Das.

Then said the jeweller: "Doubtless you have come, O Yuhanna, for the monthly subscription for the church fund and the support of the poor."

"Yes, O brother," replied Yuhanna. "I am going my rounds amongst the Christians, but as yet I have collected but little. The funds are low, and we have more sick to help and more widows to relieve than usual."

Bál Mukand, where he lay, opened his eyes a little, and he could see with what a look of pleasure his friend Shib Das drew four rupees from his store, and gave them into the hand of Yuhanna.

"It is strange, O Shib Das," observed the catechist, "that you give more to the church fund than do even baboos in government employ. You are not, I believe, a rich man. How is it that when we ask for offerings to God we never find your bag empty?"

"The reason is very simple," was Shib Das's cheerful reply. "I am a Christian, and I try to obey what is written in the Word of my God regarding offerings made unto Him: *Upon the first day of the week let every one of you lay by him in store, as God hath prospered him* (1 Cor. xvi. 2). At least a tenth of the profits of my trade I look upon as the Lord's, and not my own. Thus I ever have money at hand to give; and when I give it, I never miss it."

"God will accept your gift, and will bless you," said the catechist earnestly, ere he turned and went on his way.

And what was the thought of Bál Mukand as he lay, apparently asleep, in the innermost and darkest part of the shop? "If all men showed such piety and charity, this would be a happy land," he said in his heart. "The poverty of such men as Shib Das is better than the wealth of the worldly."

The next person who came to the shop was the bearer of a government official of rank. He carried with him a necklace which had been broken in many places. Some of the precious stones had dropped from their setting. The bearer, whose name was Parduman, showed the broken ornament to Shib Das.

"Can you mend this for the Mem Sahiba?" asked he.

Shib Das was skilful in his craft, and he said that he could certainly mend the necklace. His heart was glad, for this was the first time that the poor Christian goldsmith had been offered employment by any of the Sahib log, and it seemed to him as if God were sending prosperity to his house.

"The Mem Sahiba must have her necklace back on Monday," said the bearer, "for she is going to a grand ball on that night."

"I cannot finish the work so soon," said Shib Das, after carefully examining the broken ornament. A short time before, he would have readily made a promise, whether he had hoped to be able to keep it or not; but now that Shib Das served the God of truth, he would have suffered any loss rather than have broken his word.

"You have all to-morrow to work in," observed Parduman, the bearer.

"To-morrow is Sunday, the day set apart for worship and praise," said Shib Das. "I have given up working on that day since I have become a Christian."

Then Parduman waxed angry, and roughly took back the necklace.

"The Sahib and Sahiba are Christians," he cried, "and they do their work or take their pleasure on Sundays. Dost thou, O owl, and son of an owl, set thyself up as one wiser, or holier than they?"

"Whatever others do, I have simply to obey what is written in my sacred Book," said the Christian: "*Remember the Sabbath, to keep it holy.*"

Then Parduman, who hated all Christians, and most especially such as were real ones, burst into a torrent of abuse. Every bitter and insulting epithet that he could think of flowed from his lips, as venom from the mouth of a snake. Bál Mukand, from his dark corner, watched to see how his friend would endure the provocation which he was receiving. "Shib Das is of a fiery temper," he said to himself; "he is also strong and bold. He will give that foul-mouthed wretch sharp words back, or something sharper than words." Bál Mukand saw that the angry blood was rising to the cheek of Shib Das, and expected a burst of passion to follow. But the servant of Christ pressed his own lips firmly together, and returned not railing for railing. He only said, as his enemy, still pouring forth abuse, turned to depart, "It is a fortunate thing for you, O bearer, that I am a Christian."

"There is a strange change in this Shib Das," thought Bál Mukand. "I have known him in former days strike a man to the earth for far less provocation than this. It is assuredly not cowardice that makes him now thus calmly endure. If all men had the firmness and patience of this Shib Das, this would indeed be a happy land. The silent endurance of such men as this Christian, shows more true courage than the boldest deeds of the warrior."

Bál Mukand had but a short time to give to such reflections, for scarcely had the bearer left the jeweller's shop when the sound of a fearful scuffle was heard in the street. Three thieves of the city had gained information that Parduman had in his charge a necklace of inestimable value. Lurking near the goldsmith's shop, these thieves had heard the abuse lavished by the bearer on the Christian. While revilings and curses were yet on the lips of Parduman, he was suddenly felled to the earth by a blow. Being active and strong, he struggled again to his feet, calling out loudly for help. But the three thieves were far more than a match for the bearer. A second time he was hurled bleeding to the ground, and his wicked tongue might then have been silenced for ever, had not the brave Shib Das rushed out of his shop to the help of his enemy. The jeweller had snatched up a heavy stick on hearing Parduman's cry for help; and of this stick he made such vigorous use that the thieves were not only put to flight, but forced to leave the jewels behind them.

The care of Shib Das was then given to his wounded enemy. He offered to bind Parduman's hurts as kindly as if he had been his brother; but the Hindu declined his aid. Shib Das then brought him water to drink; but the bearer refused to take it from his hands: he would have thought himself polluted by touching with his lips the vessel of the Christian.

Bál Mukand had watched the whole scene with keen interest. "If all men were generous and forgiving as this Christian," — this was the thought of Bál Mukand, — "this would indeed be a happy land. Does yon bigoted Hindu fear pollution from the touch of Shib Das? Were the bearer not blinded by superstition, he would know that there is no caste so high and pure as that of the children of God."

Parduman left the necklace for the goldsmith to repair, — perhaps from some feeling of gratitude towards his preserver, perhaps because he feared, should he keep the jewels on his own person, to be again attacked on the road. With a bruised frame and bleeding brow Parduman left the place, and, we may hope, likewise with a humbled heart, resolved that he would not again abuse a man for being a Christian, or despise him for obeying the law of his God.

Bál Mukand had risen from his reclining posture at the first sound of the struggle in the street, though he had not, like Shib Das, rushed out to the aid of the bearer. Bál Mukand now, with a countenance full of thought, advanced towards his friend.

"O Shib Das!" he exclaimed, "said I not an hour ago that the way to the Christian's heaven was dark, and that with all my searching and reading I was not able to find it? Lo! since I entered your shop a clear light has shone on the way."

"What is your meaning, my friend?" asked the goldsmith.

"I have discovered the difference between the false flowers and the real; between those that are lifeless and those that have drunk the rain from the sky. I have seen that what is written in your Bible is true, though the words were at first an unfathomable mystery to my soul: *If any man be in Christ, he is a new creature* (2 Cor. v. 17). I have beheld the well-watered garden in which grow the fruits of honesty and truth, piety and obedience, meekness, forgiveness, and love."

"O my friend!" exclaimed Shib Das, "I am in myself weak, sinful, polluted; it is only through the death of Christ my Lord that I am saved from eternal destruction. It is only through the power of His Holy Spirit that I am enabled so much as to think one good thought."

"Having been saved, the Christian loves; and having loved, he obeys; and in obeying he glorifies God," said Bál Mukand. "Shib Das, your *example* has done for me what all your words cannot do: it has convinced me that the religion which produces such effects must be the true one; it has made me resolve to become a Christian also."

The life of every true servant of the Holy Saviour is as a lamp to light others on their way, as the blessed Lord showed when He said: *Let your light so shine before men, that they may see your good works, and glorify your Father which is in heaven* (Matt. v. 16).

IX
The Paper Parable

Three men sat conversing together in the evening, when the glowing sun had just dipped below the horizon. The names of these men were Lalla Rám, Hukam Chand, and Lajput Rai. Lalla Rám was the inhabitant of a village, and dwelt in a mud-built hut. Hukam Chand kept a little shop in a crowded lane of the city of Lahore. Lajput Rai had no settled place of abode; he was a sage who had travelled much, had seen much, had thought much, and his words were deemed words of wisdom.

The first one of the three who spoke was the villager, Lalla Rám. He had been revolving in his mind news that he had heard that day—namely, that the orphan daughter of a friend of his had been placed in a school. This was a cause of great displeasure to Lalla Rám.

"It is an evil thing," said he, "that schools for girls are now being planted over our land. Who would be so foolish as to sow corn upon a pool? Who would teach letters to a cow? Hath the sheep power to acquire knowledge? Woman was made to toil and bear burdens; she was made to labour in the field, and to grind at the mill. A book placed in the hand of a girl is as an ear-ring in the ear of an ass!"

Then spake he who dwelt in Lahore—he whose wife was ever in pardah:—"I too would close all schools for girls; but not because, in my opinion, it is good for women to labour. No: let our wives and daughters keep in pardah; and if they want amusement, let them find it in decking themselves out with jewels.[45] Women are quick enough in learning mischief without sharpening their wits by books. To put knowledge within the grasp of woman, is to put an edge-tool into the hand of a fool! Woman is only happy in ignorance, and only safe in seclusion."

"My friends," said the sage Lajput Rai, "did you ever hear the story of the rajah and the three sheets of paper?"

"No," cried Lalla Rám and Hukam Chand. "My lord, we pray you, tell us the story."

"A great rajah," began Lajput Rai, "called to him three of his servants, and committed to each of them a fair sheet of paper, upon which no letter had ever been traced. The rajah told none of the three wherefore he had given the paper, but only said, 'Use it with wisdom.' But he said to himself, 'I will judge of the understanding of each of these my servants by the use to which he shall put my gift; and he who showeth most wisdom shall receive a high place in my household.'

"After a long time had passed, the rajah again called his three servants; and after they had made their saláms, thus he spake to the first: 'To what use hast thou put that fair sheet of blank paper which I committed to thy charge, for I wish to look on it now?'

"'I wrapped seed in it, O your highness!' replied the first servant, 'and carried it into the field. The paper fell on the earth, damp with the rains, and was marred; my ox placed his foot upon it; it was trampled down into the clay. It is therefore impossible that I should lay it at your majesty's footstool.'

"Then said the rajah to his second servant, 'To what use hast thou put that goodly sheet of blank paper which I committed to thy charge, for I wish to behold it again?'

"'I put the paper to no use whatsoever, O maharajah!' replied the man, with a profound salám. 'I rolled it up, and put it carefully on a shelf in an inner apartment, where no man could see it. But the damp spotted and stained it, and the white ants fretted it; the paper is no longer fit to be looked upon by the eyes of your highness.'

"Then the rajah turned to his third servant, and said, 'To what use hast thou put that fair sheet of blank paper which I committed to thy charge?'

"Then the servant, after making obeisance, took from his bosom a roll, which he then slowly unfolded before the rajah. And lo! upon the roll, in letters of scarlet, and blue, and gold, appeared a beautiful illumination, fit for the walls of a palace. And these were the words inscribed:—*Who can find a virtuous woman? for her price is far above rubies. The heart of her husband doth safely trust in her. She will do him good and not evil all the days of her life* (Prov. xxxi. 10-12).

"'O faithful and wise servant!' cried the rajah, 'thou alone hast made a good use of my gift, thou only hast known its worth. Thou shalt reap a rich reward; and the paper which thy diligence hath made so fair, shall be framed in gold, and have an honourable place in my palace.'

"My friends," continued the sage, "see ye the meaning of my story? The blank sheets of paper are the minds of our young daughters; and he who hath trusted them to your care is the mighty King, to whom ye must one day render a strict account. Ignorance is as the treading down of the ox in the field, or as the mould that mars the roll on the shelf. *For the soul to be without knowledge is not good.* But happy the father who causes to be traced on the mind of his young daughter lessons of purity, wisdom, and truth! Those lessons shall shine forth as in characters of gold; and she who has learned in youth to serve and obey the great King, shall find an honourable place in that heaven which He hath prepared for them that love Him."

X
The Oldest Language upon Earth

The story goes that three old men—a Mohammedan, a Jew, and a Brahmin—seated on the ground beside a well, disputed together as to which was the first language spoken upon earth. The discussion waxed so hot, the voices were raised so loudly, that the sound drew to the spot a young Englishman. The youth had been out shooting; with his gun in his hand, and his game at his feet, he now stood, leaning against a tree, listening to the discussion between the three men.

The Mohammedan, with vehement gestures, and many an oath, declared that no language could equal the Arabic.

"Is it not the language," he cried, "in which Mohammed (blessed be his name!) received the holy Koran? Is it not that in which the Most High gave laws to the faithful? Will ye, O ye unbelievers! cast dust on the grave of the Prophet by doubting that Arabic is the oldest language on earth?"

The Jew shook his gray head, and his brow was knit into many wrinkles as he made answer: "The language which Abraham our father, which Isaac and Jacob (peace be on them!) spake, must be honoured above all other tongues. Surely it was heard in Paradise, before Eve plucked the forbidden fruit! The oldest and most sacred language assuredly is the Hebrew."

Then spake the Brahmin, in tones of scorn: "All languages compared to Sanscrit are as the bulrush compared with the spreading banyan. Nay; even as the banyan sends forth shoots, and from those shoots, when they touch the earth, spring forth young trees, so other tongues spring from the life-giving Sanscrit. He must be void of wisdom, and ignorant as a woman, who doubts that the most ancient language is Sanscrit."

The disputants grew so angry, that it seemed as if to words might succeed blows, when the young Englishman stepped forward.

"O venerable men!" he said with courtesy, "you have numbered many years and I but few; yet let me arbitrate between you. I know what is the most ancient and honourable language spoken on earth."

"You know!" exclaimed the Mohammedan in surprise. "You have but down upon your lips; and will you teach graybeards like us?"

The Hindu muttered to himself,—"The Sahib log think that they know everything! They can make roads and bridges, and send messages through wires; but what can they tell of ancient languages to a Brahmin?"

"The language of which I would inform you is not only the one first spoken upon earth, but it is the one now spoken in heaven," said the Englishman.

The three men stroked their beards, and uttered exclamations of astonishment at the presumption shown by the youth.

"And yet more," continued the youth, his eyes, blue as the sky, sparkling with animation as he went on,—"without learning to speak this language no man, of whatsoever nation he be, will ever be suffered to enter heaven."

"Does your honour know this language?" asked the Mohammedan quickly.

"Yes, God be praised!" the Englishman replied.

"And where did you first learn it?" asked the incredulous Jew.

In a softened tone the young man replied, "I learned it first from the lips of my mother."

The three men glanced at each other in surprise; and then the Brahmin inquired, "And what is this language, O Sahib?"

"The language of truth," said the Englishman.

When the word was spoken, the clouds cleared away from the faces of the three; they stroked their beards and cried, "Well said. Truth is the language of God; truth is the language spoken in heaven."

"But it must be learned upon earth," said the Englishman earnestly. "Before I came to this land, I gave up pleasures by day and rest by night, in order to learn the language of Hindostan. Were I not to know it, I could not remain in the honourable service to which I belong. And thus it is with truth, the language of heaven. God is truth itself, and a lie is to Him an accursed thing. It is written in His Word: *Lying lips are an abomination to the Lord.*"

Again the three men glanced at each other. There was not one of them that would not have lied for the sake of making a few pice larger profit in a bargain; lies were to them common as the mosquitoes which buzzed around their heads; not one of them had ever thought of falsehood as a deadly sin, abhorrent to God.

The Mohammedan was the one to speak first.

"Upon what authority does the Sahib affirm that the gate of heaven is closed against those who speak not the language of truth?"

"On the authority of God's holy Word, which cannot be broken," replied the Englishman. "Hear, O my friends, what is declared of the abode of the blessed by Him who cannot utter untruth: *There shall in no wise enter into it anything that defileth, neither whatsoever worketh abomination or maketh a lie.*"

"Heaven will be very empty, then," said the Jew with a sneer. "Your favoured Saint Peter, according to your own Scriptures, lied thrice, and with oaths and curses. Shall he be shut out from heaven, or shall his sin alone go unpunished?"

"Peter's sin *was* punished," replied the Englishman gravely; "but it was Peter's Lord, the Master whom Peter had denied, who bore the penalty for him. The blood that flowed from the Saviour's wounded side can wash away all sin, whether of thought or word or deed, the sin of falsehood amongst the rest. But those who would be forgiven like Peter, must, like Peter, believe and love. When God's Spirit comes into the heart, He comes to drive away evil from it; the unjust becomes just, and the proud becomes meek, and the lips that often were stained with falsehood learn the language of heaven—the language of truth."

XI
Stories on the Ten Commandments

I—THE BROKEN BRIDGE.

Hossein said to his aged grandfather Abbas, "O grandfather, wherefore are you reading the Gospel?"

Abbas made answer, "I read it, my son, to find the way to heaven."

Hossein, smiling, said, "The way is plain enough. Worship but the one true God, and keep the Commandments."[46]

The man whose hair was silvered with age made reply: "Hossein, the Commandments are as a bridge of ten arches, by which the soul might once have passed over the flood of God's wrath, and have reached heaven, but that the bridge has been shattered. There is not one amongst us that hath not broken the Commandments again and again."

"My conscience is clear!" cried Hossein proudly. "I have kept all the Commandments; at least, almost all," he added, for his conscience had given the lie to his words.

"And if one arch of a bridge give way under the traveller, doth he not surely perish in the flood, my son, though the nine others be firm and strong? But many of the arches of thy bridge are broken; yea, the very first is in ruins."

"Not the First Commandment—*Thou shalt have none other god but Me.* I have never broken that!" exclaimed Hossein indignantly. "I have never worshipped any god but one—the Almighty, the Invisible, the All-merciful. *That* arch in my bridge, at least, is whole and entire."

"The being whom we love above all others, and whose honour we most desire, the being whom we obey in all things,—is not he the one whom we worship in the temple of the heart?" inquired the old man.

"Surely; for that Being is our God!" exclaimed Hossein.

He of the silvery beard slowly rose from his seat. "Come with me, O youth," said he, "and I will show thee whom thou dost worship in the temple of thine heart."

"No man can show me Him whom I worship!" cried Hossein in indignant surprise; "for the one true God is invisible, and I worship none but Him."

"Come with me," repeated Abbas; and he led the way to a tank of water clear and pure, in which the surrounding buildings and trees were reflected as in a mirror.

Hossein followed his grandfather wondering, and saying to himself, "Age hath made the old man as one who hath lost his reason."

When the two reached the tank, Abbas said to his grandson, "Look down into the clear water, and behold him whom thou dost love above all others, whose honour thou dost most desire, whose will thou dost ever obey. O Hossein, my son! is he not to thee in the place of the one true God?"

Hossein looked down, and behold! there was his own image reflected in the clear water.

"He who loves Self more than God hath broken the first law," continued Abbas; "for is it not written: *Thou shalt love the Lord thy God with all thy heart, and with all thy soul, and with all thy mind, and with all thy strength: this is the First Commandment?* Hossein, this arch of thy bridge is broken; thou canst not pass to heaven upon it."

"And can you?" exclaimed Hossein with impatience.

"No, my son," said the old man meekly; "I have long ago seen that this, as well as other Commandments, has been broken by me, a sinner. There never was but one Man, and He the Holy One of God, with whom the bridge of obedience was perfect and entire."[47]

"If your bridge be broken, how do you hope to reach heaven at all?" inquired Hossein. "How can you, or any one else, escape being swallowed up in the flood of God's wrath?"

"By clinging to Him who cast Himself into the raging torrent that He might bear all those who believe in Him safe to the shore of heaven!" exclaimed Abbas with fervour. "Thou hast looked down on thyself, thy sinful self, O Hossein; now look upwards to Christ, the spotless One, who can save thee from self and sin. My hope of heaven is firm and sure, for it is founded on this sacred word: *God so loved the world that He gave His only begotten Son, that whoso believeth in Him should not perish, but have everlasting life."*

II — THE BURNING HUT.

Sheosahai, the Brahmin, stood in his straw-thatched cottage, gazing on the image of Krishna, the dark god, which for centuries he and his fathers had worshipped.

His young son, Sheo Deo, who from his birth had been paralyzed in his limbs, lay on his mat near, and thus addressed his father: —

"O father, the time for pujah (worship) has come! Why do you not prostrate yourself before Krishna?"

Sheosahai made reply: "My son, I was at the *mela* (fair) yesterday, and there was a man preaching;[48] and I stood to listen, and his words have troubled my soul. He said that thousands of years ago the mighty God came down upon a mountain in fire and smoke, and that from the midst of the fire and smoke a terrible voice gave this command, — *Thou shalt not make unto thyself any graven image, or the likeness of any thing that is in heaven above, or that is in the earth beneath, or that is in the water under the earth: thou shalt not bow down thyself to them.* I would fain have cast dust at the speaker; and yet his words clung to my soul, for he spake as one who knows that he speaks the truth."

"Was the great God of whom he told the God of the Christians?" asked Sheo Deo, who had heard something of their religion before.

"The same," replied his father. "And the preacher went on to say that in England, thousands of years ago, men bowed down to idols, and worshipped the work of their own hands; and then the people were feeble and few. But the nation has long since cast away idols, and now men read their holy Book, and pray to the Lord Jesus Christ; and therefore England is mighty, and a blessing rests on the land."

"O father! do you not fear the wrath of Krishna when he hears you repeat such words?" cried Sheo Deo, looking up in alarm at the painted image.

Sheosahai made no reply; he turned and slowly left the hut. Perhaps the thought arose in his heart: "Has Krishna power to hear them?"

After his father's departure Sheo Deo lay still on his mat, from which he could not move, and often he gazed up at the idol, and turned over in his mind the strange words which his father had heard.

Presently there came on a terrible storm. The thunder roared above like the noise of a thousand cannon, and fierce lightnings flashed from the darkened sky; the whole earth seemed to tremble with the fury of the great tempest.

"Was it in a storm like this," thought Sheo Deo, "that the awful voice was heard from the mountain, *Thou shalt make no graven image?*"

Then came a more terrible crash than Sheo Deo had ever before heard; and the moment after there was the smell of burning, and then the glare of fire above. Lo! the lightning had struck the hut, and the thatch was blazing over the head of the wretched boy, who, paralyzed as he was, could not even crawl out of the burning dwelling.

The red light glared on the image of Krishna; to the terrified Sheo Deo it seemed almost as if the idol had life!

"Help me—save me! Oh! save thy worshipper, great Krishna!" he cried; while the heat around him grew more and more fearful, even as that of a furnace.

But the image stirred not, heard not. The sparks were kindling upon it.

Then, in the agony of his terror, the poor Hindu bethought him of the Christian's powerful God. Even in the presence of his idol he clasped his hands and uttered the cry, "O Lord Jesus Christ, if Thou canst save me, oh! save me!"

At that moment Sheosahai burst into the blazing hut.

The Brahmin looked at his helpless boy lying on the mat, and then on the idol which he had so long worshipped. He had no time to save *both*; which should he leave to the devouring flames? Only one day previously the Hindu might have hesitated in making his choice, but he did not hesitate now. He caught up his son in his arms; he bore him forth from the fiery furnace. "If Krishna be a god he will save himself," muttered the Brahmin.

The hut was soon burned to ashes, and the idol lay a heap of cinders within it.

Sheo Deo lived; and in the following year, after much instruction from the missionary, he and his father received the water of baptism, believing that which is written in the holy Scriptures: *This is life eternal, that they might know Thee, the only true God, and Jesus Christ whom Thou hast sent.*

III—THE MARKS ON THE SAND.

A Mohammedan youth, Hakim Alí by name, on his return from a journey through Arabia, visited his friend Yuhanna, the Christian. Though the two held not the same faith, there was much friendship between them. [49] They sat together under a pépul tree, and Hakim Alí, with great animation, gave to Yuhanna an account of all that he had seen in his travels. For a long time Yuhanna had all the listening, and his friend had all the talking. In almost every sentence uttered by Hakim Alí, he brought in the name of Allah (God); if he were but describing how a mule stumbled, or what evil fare he had had at an inn, he called God to bear witness to what he said—even if he were laughing when the holy name was on his lips. Yuhanna had a stick in his hand, and every time that Hakim Alí uttered the sacred name, Yuhanna with the stick made a mark on the sand. Hakim Alí at last noticed with surprise this act of Yuhanna.

"What are you marking?" he cried.

"Debts," was the brief reply.

"You have many," laughed Hakim Alí, again using the name of the Highest; and again Yuhanna drew a line on the sand.

Then Yuhanna, turning, asked a question: "You have visited many holy shrines and sacred tombs in your life, O Hakim Alí!" said he; "did you ever take off your slippers before entering?"[50]

Hakim Alí was so much astonished at the question, that more loudly than ever he uttered the name of Allah. "Do you count me as an unclean swine?" he exclaimed; "do you doubt that I always take off my slippers on such occasions? Never without due reverence do I approach that which is holy."

Yuhanna pointed to the marks on the sand. "O my friend!" said he, "fifteen times within the last hour have you shown no reverence for that which is most holy."

"What is your meaning?" exclaimed the astonished Hakim Alí, again lightly using the sacred name of God.

Once more Yuhanna made a mark on the sand.

"Is a building made by the hands of men more to be reverenced than that sacred name before which the angels bow?" said Yuhanna gravely. "Is not every time that that name is taken in vain marked down,—not on sand, where it can be lightly effaced, but in that book of remembrance which is kept by the Highest? O my friend! it was the voice of the Almighty Himself that gave the command: *Thou shalt not take the name of the Lord thy God in vain, for the Lord will not hold him guiltless that taketh His name in vain.* This command was written first by the finger of God on the table of stone committed to Moses."[51]

"Are you Christians then so careful how you take the name of God on your lips?" asked Hakim Alí, rising somewhat angrily from his seat.

"We, of all men, should be most careful," replied his friend, "for in the prayer taught by the Lord Jesus Christ to His servants, the very first petition to God is, *Hallowed be Thy name.* If we use that name without reverence, our very prayer becomes a mockery, and we are convicted of sin before God. Solemn was the warning given by our Lord: *Every idle word that a man shall speak, he shall give account thereof in the day of judgment."*

"Who then can stand in the day of judgment?" asked Hakim Alí with a troubled countenance, as with his foot he hastily erased the marks on the sand.

"None can stand but those who can plead not their own righteousness, but the righteousness of another," replied Yuhanna, looking upwards. "Like the prophet Isaiah I have often cried: *Woe is me! for I am undone, for I am a man of unclean lips*; but when I think of the blood that was shed by Christ on the cross for sinners, to my heart the answer comes: *Lo! this hath touched thy lips, and thine iniquity is taken away, and thy sin purged. There is no condemnation to them that are in Christ Jesus."*

IV—THE BEAUTIFUL GARDEN.

There was a certain man who had a young son, Azfur Alí by name, whom he greatly loved, and whom he daily loaded with favours. One day this father said unto Azfur Alí,—"Come with me into the garden which I have purchased and prepared that it may be a goodly possession for you, O my son!"

The father then led the way to a beautiful garden, in which were all kinds of flowers,—some lovely in colour, some sweet in scent. The garden was divided into seven portions; and the flowers in the seventh portion were white as snow on the tops of the mountains.

"Now, my son, take your pleasure in six portions of this garden," said the father; "but the seventh I have kept for myself. Let not your foot wander over the border; enjoy the scent of the flowers from a little distance, but lay not a hand upon them. Behold! they are mine, and in abstaining from touching them your obedience to me shall be shown. It is my love for you, Azfur Alí, that makes me thus reserve the seventh portion. To the white flowers which blossom there on the plants will succeed a delicious fruit, to look upon which will be pleasure, and to eat which will be health. The seventh portion is to be to you even a greater blessing than the other six; but now I call it mine, so trespass not on the ground reserved."

After a while the father departed for a time to a distant place, leaving his young son behind him.

From morning till night Azfur Alí amused himself in the garden; he gathered the flowers at his pleasure, and formed wreaths of the fairest blossoms, red, yellow, and blue; but his eyes often wandered to the forbidden ground on which his feet were never to tread.

"Why should I be tied and bound down to these six portions of the garden?" cried Azfur Alí. "I do not like the scent of those white flowers; if I pulled them up, I could put in their place golden flowers that I like much better. As for the fruit of which my father spoke, I do not believe that it ever will come; at least, I cannot wait for it. A hard and unreasonable thing it is, to shut me out from a seventh part of my garden."

So Azfur Alí ran into the forbidden ground, trampling down the plants, and crushing the fair white blossoms, and some he tore up by the roots. Then he tried to put in their place plants that had golden flowers; but they flourished not, but withered, and the seventh portion of the garden was soon covered with weeds, and became a desolation!

When the father returned his wrath was great. "Azfur Alí!" he cried, "thou hast broken my command, thou hast trespassed on the seventh portion of the garden which I reserved for myself, and hast destroyed the flowers which would have borne precious fruit. Thou hast forfeited all right from henceforth to possess any part of my garden."

This story is a parable. The garden is the garden of Time, and the seventh portion is the Sabbath which the Heavenly Father hath reserved for Himself, as we read in His holy Word: *Remember the Sabbath day to keep it holy. Six days shalt thou labour, and do all thy work: but the seventh day is the Sabbath of the Lord thy God: in it thou shalt not do any work, thou, nor thy son, nor thy daughter, thy man-servant, nor thy maid-servant, thy cattle, nor thy stranger that is within thy gates: for in six days the Lord made heaven and earth, the sea, and all that in them is, and rested the seventh day: wherefore the Lord blessed the seventh day, and hallowed it.*

The white blossoms that grow in this garden are the blossoms of Prayer, and Praise, and Perusal of the Holy Scriptures. The fragrance of them is as the fragrance of the Garden of Eden. But the full sweetness of the fruit which follows will be enjoyed in heaven, where the hymn of praise on earth will be changed for the song of the Lord's redeemed: *The kingdoms of this world are become the kingdoms of the Lord and of His Christ, and He shall reign for ever and ever!*

V—THE BLIND MOTHER.

Nand Kishore was driven from his home because he had become a Christian. His dearest friends would not eat with him, or suffer him to cross their thresholds; his younger brother seized on his small property; and, worst of all, his widowed mother, Harmuzi, beating her breast, cursed her first-born, who had been to her as the apple of her eye. Then the soul of Nand Kishore was sorely smitten; in great grief he turned from the door of what had been his home from his childhood. But he remembered the words of the Saviour for whose sake he had given up all: *If any man love father or mother more than Me, he is not worthy of Me. Blessed are they that are persecuted for righteousness' sake: for theirs is the kingdom of heaven.*

Harmuzi had in her anger cursed her first-born, but her heart clung to him still. Great was her grief when, a year afterwards, she heard a report of the death of Nand Kishore. And Harmuzi had other sore trials: blindness gradually came upon her, till at last all the light of heaven to her was darkened. And her son Mohendro showed her no love or respect. He had married a proud woman, who despised her poor blind mother-in-law, and made her life bitter with cruel words. Mohendro more than once even struck[52] his afflicted mother; and Harmuzi was treated as a slave in the house which had once been her own.

"Ah! my poor Nand Kishore would not have behaved to me thus!" sighed the unhappy mother, when she remembered him whom she had cursed, only because he had done what he felt to be right.

Harmuzi's cruel daughter-in-law grudged her even the food which she ate. "Thou canst not grind the corn, or bring water from the well," she said; "and yet thou dost devour our substance. Go out into the street and beg!

When passers-by look on your blind eyes, they may at least put a handful of grain into your vessel."

Hungry and sad, and bowed down by sorrow, poor Harmuzi, wrapped in her chaddar, sat at the corner of a street, with a brass vessel, called a bartan, beside her, and held out her thin hand for alms. She had sat there for hours, whilst many passed by her, but as yet she had received nothing from any one,—not so much as a word of pity. At last Harmuzi heard a slight sound, as if something were being poured into her bartan; and when she put forth her hand to feel, lo! the vessel was full of rice. Then some one gently took the blind woman by the hand, and raised her, and led her back towards the house of the undutiful son. Harmuzi blessed the kind stranger again and again, and asked Vishnu to load him with blessings. He who led her spake not a word in reply, but left her at the corner of a street that was nigh to the house of her undutiful son.

The next day Harmuzi was again driven forth by her daughter-in-law to beg, and felt her way slowly to the same spot where the merciful stranger had found her. This time she had not to wait so long. Again was her bartan filled with rice, again the same gentle hand led the blind woman back; and she blessed him who had showed her mercy. But the stranger spake no word in reply.

And this went on for many days. The supply of rice never failed, and Harmuzi knew not that he who filled her bartan often himself hungered that she might be fed. Harmuzi marvelled that she never heard the sound of the stranger's voice. "He hath been smitten with dumbness," she said to herself.

One day poor Harmuzi, with bruise marks on her face, sat in her usual place; she was bitterly weeping, for the hand of her wicked younger son had been lifted up against his blind and helpless mother. At the sight of Harmuzi's bruises and tears, he who had so long restrained himself[53] could keep silence no longer.

"O mother—mother!" he cried. Harmuzi knew the voice of her lost Nand Kishore, and suddenly rising and stretching out her arms, she fell on his neck weeping.

"O my beloved!" she cried, "is it thou? How is it that thou hast so long fed and cared for her who, in an evil hour, cursed her own first-born son?"

"Dear to my soul!" replied Nand Kishore, "do you not know that He who said, *He that loveth father or mother more than Me, is not worthy of Me,* also gave this command, *Honour thy father and thy mother, that thy days may be long upon the land which the Lord thy God giveth thee?*"

VI—A DANGEROUS VILLAGE.

Padre Ware, a missionary, revisited a village in which four heads of families, whose names were Nihal, Tara Chund, Chanda Lal, and Lala, had received the gospel, and been baptized. After an absence of six months Padre Ware returned to the village, hoping to find the four Christians firm in the faith, and glorifying by their holy lives the Saviour whom they had promised to serve. Alas! great was the sorrow of Padre Ware to find that Satan had sown the seeds of discord and hatred amongst the little band who should have loved one another, even as Christ had loved them. Nihal had a quarrel with Tara Chund about a bit of land; Chanda Lal's wife had said bitter things against Lala's. None of the four would speak with his neighbour. Even the coming of Padre Ware was a fresh cause of bitterness. Each one of the four men asked the missionary to abide in his house; the Englishman could not go to the one without offending the other three. Where Padre Ware had hoped to find love and peace and joy, he found anger, hatred, and strife.

Under the shade of a banyan-tree sat Padre Ware, with his Bible in his hand; and thither, to meet him, came Nihal, Tara Chund, Chanda Lal, and Lala,—but they sat on the ground as far apart as they could from each other. Many of the villagers stood at a little distance to see the missionary, and listen to his words; but none of these villagers wished to become Christians, for they said amongst themselves: "Padre Ware, when he was here before, told us that God is love, and Christ's religion a religion of love; but behold these men who have been baptized, they will not so much as eat together!"

Padre Ware looked sadly upon the four converts who were thus bringing dishonour on the name of Christians. For a few moments he lifted up his heart in prayer for them, and then he spoke aloud:—

"It is the desire of my heart that all may be peace and love between you. Nihal is the oldest amongst you: let us all go to his house, and take a meal together, in token that all again are friends."

But Tara Chund shook his head and cried, "Never will I cross the threshold of Nihal!" And Chanda Lal and Lala looked fiercely at each other, and muttered, "We never will eat together."

Then said Padre Ware to the four: "I have been for twelve years a missionary. I have gone in and out amongst the people; I have never refused to go to the house of him who invited me, nor to eat with any who was willing to eat with me. Only once was I in a great difficulty: I went to one village where several were ready indeed to receive me, but I knew that they all were murderers."

"All murderers!" exclaimed the astonished Christians. "That was an evil place indeed."

"What was I to do?" asked Padre Ware.

All the four answered as with one breath,—"Get out of that village as fast as your honour could."

Then Padre Ware opened his Bible, and slowly read: *Whosoever hateth his brother is a murderer, and ye know that no murderer hath eternal life abiding in him.*

There was a great silence, and then the missionary went on:—"O my friends! ye know that God hath commanded, *Thou shalt not kill*; and His Word hath shown us that this command reaches even to the thoughts of the heart. Ye call yourselves servants of that Saviour who loved His enemies, prayed for His enemies, died for His enemies; but oh! remember that they who come to Him for pardon and life, must also follow Him in holiness and love,—for is it not written in the Scriptures of truth, *If any man have not the Spirit of Christ, he is none of His*"? (Rom. viii. 9).

Again there was a deep silence. Then Nihal arose from the ground, and going up to Tara Chund, offered his hookah;[54] and Tara Chund accepted it with a smile. The four Christians embraced one another; and before the evening closed in, those who had been bitter enemies ate together as friends and brethren in Christ.[55]

VII—THE BEAUTIFUL PARDAH.

It is quite necessary to give a few words of introduction to the following little story, as without it the meaning and drift of it would be quite unintelligible to many British readers. Not all are aware that it is the custom of Mohammedans of the upper classes to seclude their women from sight; so that to allow the face to be seen by any man except a husband or very near relative is accounted a shame and disgrace. This custom is called "pardah," and it has spread beyond the Mohammedans to some of the Hindus, &c. A. L. O. E. has seen an old lady start from her seat as if in great alarm, and hide herself behind a chair, because an aged gentleman had chanced to come in sight. Sometimes sufferers are shut out from receiving medical aid on account of pardah. At this moment pardah is one of the greatest obstacles to baptism being received by one whom we believe to be quite convinced of the truth of Christianity, and whose husband is a noble-hearted Christian. Sometimes pardah is actually kept up by native *converts*; and this is a grievous hindrance to them, and besets their path with needless difficulties. There is in our mission church a little pardah room, indeed, in which women can, if they wish it, hear unseen; but how can a woman in pardah ever share the Holy Communion—how can she be actively useful amongst the heathen around her! Pardah is the napkin under which a few native converts would hide their talent, and one cannot but regard it rather as a kind of *fashion*, a piece of Oriental worldliness, than a token of superior delicacy of mind. A woman actually in the act of hiding her face will sometimes shock our feelings of refinement in some other way.

Another little explanation is necessary. The word "pardah"[56] has two meanings: one the state of seclusion which has been described; the other, the *curtain* which is the emblem of seclusion. Any curtain in an English lady's dwelling is a pardah, though she is never "in pardah" herself.

Waziren, a merchant's wife, came to visit Maryam, the wife of a moonshee. Both of the women had been baptized as Christians, but the heart of Waziren still clung to many of the customs of her people; she retained prejudices in which she had been brought up from her childhood. Waziren never came to church, lest she should break pardah; and would have thought it unseemly to meet at a meal even the dearest friend of her husband. Waziren cared not to learn to read; her only pleasure was in her jewels, and in gossip, in which her favourite topic always was the faults of her neighbours. It was for the sake of talking over news that Waziren now took her seat on the *charpai* (low bed) of Maryam.

"Are the tidings true," asked Waziren, "that your next-door neighbour, Shadi Shah, arrived last night from England, a week before he was expected?"

"It is quite true," Maryam replied. "It was a great joy to Fatima to see her husband again after a six months' absence."

"A great joy, was it?" said Waziren sneeringly; and she smiled an unpleasant smile. "I should have thought that Fatima would have cared little if the absence of her husband had been one of six years, instead of six months."

Maryam looked almost angry, for she saw that evil thoughts were in the mind of her neighbour. "Fatima is a good and faithful wife," she replied. "Had Shadi Shah remained away for six years, he would, on his return, have found her just the same as if he had never left her. Do you not know, O Waziren! that Fatima has kept in strict pardah all the time of her husband's absence?"

"In pardah!" exclaimed the astonished Waziren. "Now, for once, O Maryam! I have found you uttering words of untruth! I happen to know that Fatima has been to church every week since her husband's departure. I am sure that she on foot has visited friends; nay, I have even heard that she has taught in a school!" Waziren looked duly indignant and shocked at such a breach of Oriental customs, though quite aware that Maryam did all the things which she professed to think so strange.

"Fatima has done all this," replied Maryam, smiling; "and yet she has kept strict pardah."

"You amaze me!" cried the merchant's wife.

"Perhaps you have never heard that in Fatima's house there is a very fine pardah, beautiful and perfect, though of great antiquity," said Maryam. "This pardah is more valuable than any shawl or Cashmere, or piece of golden embroidery, crusted all over with jewels!"

"I think that you must have lost your wits!" exclaimed Waziren, more and more astonished. "I know no woman with fewer jewels than Fatima. I am sure that she cannot love her stingy husband. If she has such a splendid pardah, she never had it from him. Pray, have you ever seen this wonderful pardah?"

"Yes; and I have one just like it," replied Maryam, laying her hand on a book beside her, which Waziren, though she could not read it, knew to be the Bible.

"You talk in riddles!" cried the merchant's wife.

Maryam opened the Holy Book. First, she found out in the Old Testament the seventh commandment; and then she turned over to the New Testament and read aloud: *I will therefore that women adorn themselves in modest apparel, with shamefacedness and sobriety; not with broided hair, or gold, or pearls, or costly array; but (which becometh women professing godliness) with good works* (1 Tim. ii. 9, 10). Then from another place the Christian woman read: *Likewise, ye wives, be in subjection to your own husbands; that, if any obey not the word, they may be won by the conversation of the wives; while they behold your chaste conversation coupled with fear* (1 Peter iii. 1).

And then again Maryam found that place where that word is written alike for men and women: *Follow peace with all men, and holiness, without which no man shall see the Lord* (Heb. xii. 14). "Behold," cried Maryam, closing the Bible, "here is the pardah treasured in the house and heart of Fatima; and as long as she keeps within it, the Christian wife requires no other!"

VIII — THE BEARER'S DREAM.

Ganesh Das, the Commissioner Sahib's Sardar bearer, sat with the Bible on his knee; for Ganesh Das could read, and he had been well instructed in the Christian religion. He was convinced that that religion is true, but he loved it not, because it also is pure and holy. Ganesh Das had read the commandment, *Thou shalt not steal* (Ex. xx. 15); his finger was now on the words: *Exhort servants to be obedient to their own masters, and to please them well in all things; not answering again; not purloining, but shewing all good fidelity; that they may adorn the doctrine of God our Saviour in all things* (Titus ii. 9, 10). Ganesh Das with vexation closed the Bible and pushed it aside.

"What!" he cried; "must I, if I be baptized, give up all cheating, get nothing but my pay, never take from my rich master one pie that is not lawfully mine! No, no; this is more than I can do! Let others be Christians, — Ganesh Das cannot break off from the habit of years, and make himself poor for the sake of the gospel!"

That night Ganesh Das had a dream. He dreamed that he and many others stood in a slave-market, heavily chained, and the voice of wailing was heard around. One who wore a black robe stood near, and to him Ganesh Das addressed this question, —

"Why are we chained here? What hath brought us into this place of shame and sorrow?"

"O lost one!" replied the stranger, "thou and all around thee have been sold to a fearful tyrant, who, after ye have done his work, will cast you into devouring flames, for thus he always treats his slaves when their time of labour for him is ended."

"How came we to be slaves? What villain hath sold us?" exclaimed the indignant Sardar.

"O man!" the stranger replied, "no one is here that hath not sold himself into bondage; and lo! the money which he hath received in exchange for his soul is now the chain with which he is bound. Fools, fools! hath not Christ said: *What shall it profit a man, if he gain the whole world, and lose his own soul? Or what shall a man give in exchange for his soul?"* (Mark viii. 36.)

Even as he spoke there was a fearful noise of drums, mingled with shrieks and howlings: the tyrant was coming to the slave-market to claim his victims.

Ganesh Das in his dream trembled exceedingly, for never had he beheld a form so horrible as that which he looked on now. The glare of the enemy's eyes was as the glare of the tiger's when he rangeth the jungle at night for his prey. The tyrant advanced to the first of the slaves, and Ganesh Das saw a poor wretch crouching down in extreme terror at the feet of the soul-destroyer.

Then he of the black robe said: "Behold! this wretch is a mighty vizier, who became wealthy as a rajah through the bribes which he took. Look at the gold and the jewels which bind him now, so that he cannot so much as look up!"

Ganesh Das looked, and behold the golden chains were eating into the very flesh of the man who had sold himself to the soul-destroyer.

"He is mine!" cried the tyrant; "bear him away!"

Then he advanced to the slave who was next to Ganesh Das,—a man who stood with his eyes almost starting from his head with terror, whilst he vainly tried to burst fetters made of silver rupees.

"This is a dacoit,"[57] said he of the black robe; "he hath sold himself for the silver chain which thou seest."

"He is mine!" cried the tyrant; "bear him away!"

"I shall be next," thought the terrified dreamer. He looked down on his own galling chains, and lo! they were formed of innumerable pice and pies, the fruit of petty frauds for which he had sold his soul. The destroyer approached; the trembling Sardar seemed already to hear the doom, "He is mine! bear him away!" The poor wretch made so desperate an effort to burst his chains, that lo! he awoke from his dream.

Ganesh Das still trembled, but he was thankful that his day of grace was not yet past, that it was not yet too late to escape the soul-destroyer. He fell on his knees, repeating words which he had learned from the Bible: *Let the wicked forsake his way, and the unrighteous man his thoughts: and let him return unto the Lord, and He will have mercy upon him; and to our God, for He will abundantly pardon* (Isa. lv. 7). *For the wages of sin is death; but the gift of God is eternal life through Jesus Christ our Lord* (Rom. vi. 23).

IX—THE CRACKED SCENT-BOTTLE.

Mohendro, the Padre Sahib's bearer, saw that Melo, the Mem Sahiba's new ayah,[58] had a troubled countenance.

"Why are you troubled, Melo?" asked he.

"When dusting the Mem Sahiba's room," replied Melo, "I threw down her beautiful scent-bottle. The scent-bottle was cracked, and the sweet water was all spilt."

"What matters it to you?" said the bearer, smiling. "You have been but one day in the house; put the bottle back in its place, and when the Mem Sahiba sees that it has been emptied and cracked, say that you found it so, and that the last ayah certainly did the mischief."

A short time before, Melo would have thought nothing of telling a lie; but she was now a baptized Christian, and had been taught God's Commandments. Melo knew that one of them is, *Thou shalt not bear false witness against thy neighbour* (Ex. xx. 16). Melo had resolved to keep a strict watch over her lips, for she had learned the text: *Lying lips are abomination to the Lord* (Prov. xii. 22). "I am afraid to tell my Mem Sahiba a lie," she replied.

The bearer laughed at her words. "Why, to lie comes as natural as to eat!" he cried. "The last ayah has gone away to Benares, so your lie will do no harm to any one in the world."

Melo thought to herself, "Will it do no harm to myself?" But Melo was but a new Christian; habit is strong, and she had been accustomed to tell lies from the time that she first could speak. Melo resolved that when her Mem Sahiba noticed the harm done to the scent-bottle, she would say that the last ayah had done it. She was timid, and could not bear that the Mem Sahiba, whose service she had just entered, should think her careless.

The Padre Sahib had morning prayers in Urdu, and such of his servants as were Christians were always allowed to attend. It was the first time that Melo had ever been present at family worship. She sat on the carpet, watching the Sahib as he unclosed the Holy Book. On the knees of the Mem Sahiba sat her little boy Henry, a lovely blue-eyed child of four years of age.

The Sahib read about heaven; of the bright happy home of those who have believed in the Lord Jesus Christ, and who, believing, have loved and obeyed Him. Melo did not know this part of the Bible at all. She listened with delight to the account of the glorious place, till the reader came to the following words:—*And there shall in no wise enter into it anything that defileth, neither whatsoever worketh abomination, or maketh a lie* (Rev. xxi. 27).

Melo was startled to hear this. "Shall I be shut out from heaven?" she said to herself. But Melo could not even yet make up her mind to tell her Mem Sahiba all the truth about her beautiful scent-bottle.

When prayers were over, Melo was ordered to take Baba Henry into the garden; for it was the cold season, and the weather was not yet too hot. Melo loved children very much, and it was with pleasure that she watched the gambols of the fair little English boy.

Henry ran about the garden, and in his play he forgot to keep to the gravel path. Carelessly running across the border, the child brushed past a beautiful flower which he knew that his mother greatly prized, and in doing so broke off its head. The child stood still at once, and looked with vexation at the mischief which he had done.

"Oh! mamma told me not to run over the border, or to touch the flowers! She will be so vexed!" cried the child, almost bursting into tears.

"Never mind, Baba Henry," said Melo; "you need say nothing to the Mem Sahiba about the matter."

The boy looked indignantly into the face of the ayah with his steady blue eyes. "If I did not tell the truth, God would be angry," he cried; and off darted the child, to confess everything to his mother.

Melo looked after him, and tears came into her eyes. "Shall that little one fear God and speak truth?" she exclaimed; "and shall I, who have given myself to the God of truth, tell lies like a heathen? O Lord! help me to put away this great sin!" And quickly Melo followed her little charge, and confessed to her Mem Sahiba that she had thrown down and cracked her bottle.

And was the Mem Sahiba angry? No; her words were: "I thank God that I have at last a servant whose word I can trust."

X—THE FALL, THE CHEETAH, AND THE CUP.

Jai Singh, a man of good family, but poor, stood by the side of the road as Parduman, once his boyhood's companion, rode by. Parduman was mounted on an Arab horse of great value, richly caparisoned; and two syces attended their master. Envy and covetousness awoke in the heart of Jai Singh as he gazed.

"Why should that fellow have all life's honey, and I he left the gall?" he exclaimed. "Would that your horse were mine; ay, and the heavy bags of rupees also, that have fallen to the lot of one less worthy than myself to possess them!"

"O my son, beware of desiring that which is another's!" said Isaac, the aged catechist, who had been a friend and teacher of Jai Singh from his childhood, and who, chancing to be near, had overheard the exclamation. "In the Word of God it is written: *Thou shalt not covet thy neighbour's house, thou shalt not covet thy neighbour's wife, nor his man-servant, nor his maid-servant, nor his ox, nor his ass, nor any thing that is thy neighbour's*" (Ex. xx. 17).

"What matters the thought, if the act be blameless?" inquired Jai Singh. "I will never lift up my hand to steal or to slay."

"As the seed to the plant, as the crocodile's egg to the living reptile, so is the thought of the heart to the deed of the hand," answered old Isaac. "Man seeth the action, God searcheth the heart. In God's sight he that hateth, murders; and he that coveteth, steals. It is written in the Bible: *The love of money is the root of all evil* (1 Tim. vi. 10). Dig up the root, and no poisonous fruits can appear."

Jai Singh shrank from the purity of such a religion as this, which must convict all men of sin before God. Rather impatiently he said, "Unless evil be seen, I deny that it is evil at all."

"Hear an incident of my life which has been to me as a parable," said old Isaac. "Before I had one white hair in my beard, I went on a journey in a mountainous part of our land. Going up a steep place, my horse stumbled and threw me, and I fell down a precipice; but my dress caught in some bushes, and though hurt I was able to regain the road and again mount my horse. Riding on again, I had not gone far when a cheetah burst from the thicket, and suddenly sprang upon me. I was a strong man then, and carried a sharp knife in my girdle; after a struggle the cheetah was killed, but I bear on me the marks of its claws to this day. Weary and weakened by the loss of blood, I was forced to stop at the nearest house, though it was the house of one whom I had known as a deadly enemy. He received me with sullen looks, but denied me not rest nor food. He brought to me a cup of wine, and I drank it; I knew not that there was poison in the cup. The evil that I saw not, O Jai Singh! was worse than the more startling dangers through which I had passed. I suffered more from the poison hidden in my frame, than from the fall down the precipice, or the claws of the cheetah."

"How is it that you are here to-day, if you were poisoned?" inquired Jai Singh.

"When, after leaving my enemy's house, I arrived at the place for which I was bound," replied Isaac, "I was in sore sickness and pain; but I found there a doctor of great skill, who gave me a powerful antidote, and after much suffering I rose from my sick-bed healed. And from the Christian doctor I also received knowledge of the only antidote for sin,—whether it be the open sin which man condemns, or the poison of sin, such as covetousness, lying concealed in the heart."

"He taught you Christianity," observed Jai Singh.

"He taught me that for all past sin there is one remedy freely offered by God to all who truly believe: *The blood of Jesus Christ His Son cleanseth us from all sin* (1 John i. 7). But we need more than to be saved from the punishment of sin; we need to be saved from its power. The heart, the seat of evil, must itself be made pure by the Holy Spirit of God. And this Spirit is promised in answer to prayer. Let us cry, with David in the psalm: *Create in me a clean heart, O God, and renew a right spirit within me* (Psalm li. 10). For thus spake the Saviour of mankind: *If ye, being evil, know how to give good gifts to your children: how much more shall your heavenly Father give the Holy Spirit to them that ask Him?*" (Luke xi. 13.)

FOOTNOTES

[1]   A kind of large Oriental pipe.

[2]   One of the difficulties experienced in writing for natives is the selection of names. The Hindus, Sikhs, and Mohammedans have all *quite different sets of names*; and to give one member of a family a Mohammedan, and another a Hindu name, would be a very serious mistake in an author. A government inspector of schools has very kindly supplied A. L. O. E. with carefully arranged lists of names.

[3]   An enormous kind of fan swung across the room, the motion of which renders the heat more supportable.

[4]   A rupee is worth less than two shillings.

[5]   A name for the houses of European gentlemen.

[6]   A name commonly given to missionaries.

[7]   English gentleman.

[8]   The common form of greeting, meaning, "Peace be to you."

[9]   Note.

[10]   As not even the missionaries knew in what manner a woman of good family would address her husband, a native was consulted on the question. In Amritsar we have the advantage of having a converted Brahman on the one side, and a converted Mohammedan of position on the other, from whom we can gather information on such matters.

[11]   Husbandmen.

[12]   A small copper coin.

[13]   A very beautiful marble building in Agra.

[14]   The pugree worn by natives in the Punjaub, both old and young, is often formed of many yards of a very light material, wrapped round and round so as to form a turban. The pugree worn by Europeans as a protection from the heat is much smaller, and worn in a different manner.

[15]   A moonshee is a teacher of languages. The moonshee employed by A. L. O. E. on her first arrival in Amritsar was a convert from Mohammedanism, and a noble specimen of the class.

[16]   A baboo is one of an upper class; the title in this part of India somewhat resembles our "Mr."

[17]   This is no fictitious picture of the trials of some of the converts.

[18]   A very common word used to describe any grand show or scene of excitement.

[19]   Yuhanna (John) is a Christian name. On receiving baptism, sometimes a new name is adopted; sometimes, as with Hassan, the old one is retained.

[20]   Title given to a native lady.

[21]   Groom.

[22]   Native pony.

[23]   The natives of India like to expend large sums on such occasions, even if they plunge themselves deep into debt to defray the expenses.

[24]   Custom; a word which has far more force in India than in England.

[25]   A kind of bracelet.

[26]   The love of Indian women for ornaments must not be measured by that of English maidens. There is nothing very remarkable here in the sight of a woman wearing at one time *twelve* ear-rings, at least as many bracelets, besides necklace, nose-ring, anklets, and silver plates on her toes! Converts do not wear so many.

[27]   The chaddar (literally sheet) is a garment not worn in all parts of India, but very commonly in the Punjaub. It is something like a large veil, made of muslin or some other light material, and is worn in the house as well as out of it. Anything more graceful, picturesque, and modest-looking can hardly be imagined.

[28]   English lady.

[29]   Those conversant with India need not be told that a fearful want of truthfulness prevails amongst the natives. Against this evil the attention of missionaries has been earnestly

directed, and in some cases with great success. A. L. O. E. heard since her arrival a story of a school in Calcutta (she believes, however, that it was a Eurasian school). A prize was offered in it for truthfulness, and as it would have been almost impossible for a teacher to have adjudged the prize to the satisfaction of all, to the girls themselves the decision was left. All the children fixed upon one of their companions as the most truthful girl in the school. The wisdom of their choice was shown by the conscientious girl's declining to accept the prize, for she did not think herself *truthful enough* to deserve it!

[30] The first native of India who saw the translation of this little story—a refined and educated man—was much struck by the new view presented to him of his parental duty. He actually, very shortly afterwards, *punished his child for telling a lie*. The little boy was probably surprised at receiving chastisement for what is usually deemed such a very trifling offence; but the punishment (not a severe one) seemed to have made an impression on his young mind. Soon afterwards, on his sister asking him whether something which he had said were true, the child, with a new sense of the evil of falsehood, said, "Do you not know that God is angry when we tell lies?"

[31] The worshippers of various heathen deities may be distinguished by differently shaped marks on their foreheads.

[32] The Ganges is regarded as a peculiarly sacred river.

[33] In India, as in France, it is very uncourteous to use the third person singular Where I am, even servants are addressed as "you."

[34] In happy England, the difficulty of crossing the river of Baptism to many converts in India can hardly be appreciated. To do so is to pass the Rubicon, to cut the tie which connects the believer with all that was dear upon earth, to cast away honour, friendship, enjoyment; it is indeed to take up the Cross! One of our noblest Punjaubi Christians lingered five years before he was given courage to cross the river. One youth was brought into court to declare whether it was his deliberate choice to become a Christian. His mother drew forth a knife, and told her son that if he were baptized she

would plunge it into her own bosom! I have seen another youth who could well bear witness to the sharpness of the thorns of Persecution. His own father made him stand in *boiling oil*, till the skin was burnt off his poor feet! But he has crossed the river.

[35] A tendency to fatalism in the Oriental character is one of the great difficulties with which missionaries have to contend. It gives to the timid convert an excuse for indolence and apathy. "If it be God's will, I shall have the blessing," he thinks or professes to think "without making any struggle to obtain it."

[36] Oriental pipe.

[37] Probably at least a dozen.

[38] *The sin which doth so easily beset us.* — Heb. xii. 1.

[39] Let not the meaning of my little parable be misunderstood. Even the true believer must expect many assaults of Temptation, many a struggle with besetting sin. The pearl, Purity, is perfected only in a brighter world. Nevertheless, not only Christ's imputed righteousness, but a *growing likeness* to Him who said, "Learn of Me," is one of God's free gifts to His children through the indwelling of His Spirit. It is particularly necessary to enforce this truth in a land like India, where even sincere converts find it very hard to lead *consistent* lives, after having been brought up in the paths of sin.

[40] Native Christian parents are here intended, some of whom send their children to schools conducted by missionaries.

[41] The character of Ghuldasta has been drawn from Indian life; some of our little British maidens may, however, find that some of its features are by no means confined to girls of Hindostan.

[42] This hymn (translated) is a great favourite in this country. Even heathen and Mohammedan children like to sing it, as well as native Christians.

[43] This is a natural view to be taken by one half persuaded, who would make the inconsistencies of professed believers an excuse for not joining their ranks. It is but fair, however, to the native Christians, for whom this tale was specially

written, to say that their standard of morality is much higher than that which is adopted by their heathen neighbours.

[44] An anna is about three half-pence. There are twelve pies in an anna.

[45] The quantity of ornaments worn by women even of the humbler classes is at first surprising to a European. A woman will in *one ear* wear eight or ten rings, and as many bracelets on each arm. Her feet, also, are frequently adorned.

[46] It will be observed by those who know the East that Hossein was a Mohammedan, and not an idolatrous Hindu. In India there are different religions, not only varying from, but actually opposed to each other. Many Mohammedans in India have a considerable amount of religious knowledge.

[47] Abbas was, of course, a native Christian.

[48] These *melas* afford grand opportunities to the missionary, both for preaching and selling books.

[49] A. L. O. E. has herself heard a Mohammedan speak of Christian converts as his friends. She is on terms of affectionate intercourse with Mohammedan ladies.

[50] Not to do so is a mark of great disrespect. A native on entering a gentleman's house leaves his slippers at the door.

[51] Moses is reverenced by Mohammedans as well as by Christians.

[52] When my friend Mrs. E. was staying in a Punjaubi village, she was shocked to hear of one of the natives having beaten his mother. When she said that in England such a sin would be punished, her observation excited *general amusement*. Why should she be shocked at an event of such common occurrence?

[53] The convert probably restrained himself lest his mother should refuse to accept from his polluted touch even food needful to save her from starvation. But with the blind woman nature was too strong even for Hindu prejudice.

[54] Offering the hookah (a kind of pipe) was an alteration suggested by one who has intimate acquaintance with Oriental customs. The words originally stood: "Held out his hand; and Tara Chund grasped it," &c. This would have made the whole story unnatural.

[55]   This little story is founded on what really happened in a village not very far from Amritsar, but the words which produced a reconciliation were really spoken by one of the four who had quarrelled. A. L. O. E. heard a graphic account of the scene from a gentleman who had been present. That the reconciliation was not merely outward, seems to be proved by the fact that some little time afterwards the four Christian villagers came in a body and partook of the Holy Communion in the mission church of Amritsar.

[56]   Pronounced *purdah*.

[57]   Robber.

[58]   Female attendant.